Immortal

Adam Nicke

Adam Nicke was born near Caerleon in Wales on the Lupercalia, and just a few miles from where the Gothic author Arthur Machen was born in 1863.

In his early twenties, his artistic tendencies were expressed in the designing and making of clothes, most notably for Wayne Hussey of The Mission.

In 2015, after being plagued by years of depression and being told that nothing but counselling would help, he collapsed and underwent neurosurgery for the removal of a previously undiagnosed tennis ball-sized brain tumour.

He has a Bachelor of Arts degree in Literary Studies from the University of the West of England. His thesis was written on The Metamorphosis of the Devil in Legend and Literature.

Adam Nicke Publishing

Reviews left on Amazon or Goodreads help promote the books you love.

Published by Adam Nicke Publishing, 2021
adamnicke@gmail.com

Cover design by Adam Nicke
Imprint: Independently published

ISBN-13: 9798748111171 (Paperback)

Contents

Chapter One

Cassandra Wyvern hadn't been at her friend, Anna Harris', house for very long before the floodgates of frustration opened.

"Why should I feel embarrassed to say that I'm a woman who enjoys sex?" said Cassandra.

"You shouldn't, babe," said her friend, Anna.

"Thank you! Simeon makes me feel like a slut if I suggest something new. I don't even enjoy sex with him as his idea of foreplay is me giving him a blowjob! He won't even try a sixty-nine with me as he says – and I quote – 'I'm not licking a drain'," Cassandra said, rolling her eyes and shaking her fists at the heavens in exasperation.

"The cheeky bastard," Anna said, widening her eyes in shock. "Let's have a glass of wine and go into the garden - and we can set the world right."

"Only the one? After the sex I'm getting, I need a bottle! Haven't you got any gin?"

"A drop of mother's ruin? Why not!" Anna laughed, opening a bottle of gin before going to her fridge for a bottle of tonic water.

Chapter One

"He also tells me he can do better than me," Cassandra said.

"I've never met this guy, Cass, but he'd had to be pretty special to get someone better than you."

"Thank you," Cassandra replied. "He tells me I'm ugly."

"What a crock of crap!" Anna said. "You look like Shannyn Sossamon – and she's beautiful."

"Thank you, that's very kind of you – but doesn't she have short hair?"

"She has long hair in a few movies but I was talking about her face. God, the things I'd like to do to her!" said Anna.

The two women made their way from Anna's kitchen, through her dining room and out on to her patio.

"I don't want to brag but my sex life is great!" Anna said, sitting down on a bench attached to her picnic table.

"Sex life? If it wasn't for my vibrator, I don't think I'd have a sex life! Sex with Simeon leaves me feeling frustrated as it's just a few minutes of him grunting away, pulling a face like he's drunk

Chapter One

a glass of vinegar, rolling off, then telling me it was great. Well, no, it was crap. I want to be seduced, kissed, touched. I want every part of me to want sex. I want to know I'm the only one he's thinking of when we're doing it and that the look he has on his face is because he's doing it with me. He makes me feel like anyone would do, he's just doing it with me as I happen to be there and it's easier than spending a night down the pub on a Saturday night trying to pull."

"Except he can't even do that because of the lockdown," Anna interjected.

"Exactly! This lockdown has made it even worse as we're stuck with each other. The only time we go out is when we go to the supermarket. I swear, much more of this and I'll be passing a note to that old fella on the checkout asking him if he fancies giving me a seeing to on his conveyor belt!"

Both women laughed at the thought of Cassandra's libido driving her to such a desperate measure.

"Was it always crap between the two of you?" Anna asked. Lockdown had now been in place for a year and while Cassandra had been

Chapter One

with her partner for a little while longer than that they had only been in a relationship for a few months before the pandemic lockdown began.

"Honestly?" Cassandra asked, brushing her dark hair from her face, and looking at her friend.

"Yes," Anna replied, knowing that Cassandra would tell her sooner or later, whatever her response. Cassandra and Anna had met at university and had, at one time, enjoyed a few lesbian trysts with one another. Anna enjoyed Cassandra's company as she was always honest with her.

"Yes. I knew internet dating wasn't a good move. Jo was saying that if they're such a great catch then why are they having to advertise themselves? What's more, you don't know their history or why the women in their town are giving them the cold shoulder. He was the best of the lot. God, remember the one with no teeth? And the one with dirty fingernails that spent the date rolling his own cigarettes and spitting tobacco at me!"

"Yes, and the one you thought had trodden in something, only it was him!"

Chapter One

"Oh God, I'd forgotten about him!" laughed Cassandra.

"But just because the one you're with now is the best of a bad lot, it doesn't mean he's the one for you," said Anna, returning the conversation to Cassandra's current partner and giving her friend's hand a caring squeeze.

"I know, but it now feels like we're stuck with one another. I gave up my flat because I believed him when promised me the earth. He's made it more and more difficult to see my friends. The lockdown was a gift to him," Cassandra said, pausing to collect her thoughts and taking a large gulp of gin and tonic. "The sex was never great but I thought it would get better once we loved one another and got used to what we like and don't like but, if anything, it's worse," she said, pausing to think. "It's not fulfilling - sometimes I feel like I'm just letting him do it as any sex is better than no sex. I now feel trapped as I don't have money, a job, or even a place of my own. I'm stuck with it," she added, then sighing and brushing her hair from her face.

Chapter One

Anna took a large sip of her gin and tonic and made herself comfortable on the wooden bench.

"I know it's no consolation but I'm having the best sex ever," Anna said.

"Ever?" Cassandra asked.

"Well, the best sex I've ever had with a man!"

"That's better!" Cassandra said, both women giggling as they remembered the nights that they had spent with one another.

"Remember the idiots we slept with at university? A few drinks, a grope and a fondle with some twerp that was too drunk to even undo a bra!" Anna said, slapping her thigh and laughing.

"Remember? I'm still having sex like that! Just last night he got so drunk he couldn't manage it," Cassandra replied.

"Like playing pool with a length of rope instead of a cue? Yes, been there – and bought the t-shirt!"

The sun had gone behind clouds as the women had entered the garden but now that those clouds had moved the two women were suddenly

Chapter One

bathed in a warming amber caress. Cassandra reached for her bag and, after a moment's rummaging, removed her sunglasses.

"I wish I'd never moved to Wales," she said. "I think leaving Bristol and crossing that Severn Bridge was one of the worst decisions I've ever made," she added, as she put on her shades.

"Aw, don't say that. I'm here. Get out in the pretty valleys, the mountains, and the forests - it's a place of myth and magic!"

"Yes, but you're one of the few people I know, other than Simeon and his moron friends," Cassandra sighed. "Speaking of myth and magic, did you know that Wales and Wallachia have something in common? Both their names come from the old word *walhaz* – the strangers."

"There you go, you always said you wanted to meet someone mysterious," Anna said, giving her friend's shoulder a playful push.

"You do make me laugh, Anna! Why can't I find a man like you?"

"Well, who needs men?" Anna replied.

"Well, it would be nice to be kissed now and again."

Chapter One

"Then give me a kiss," Anna said, her jollity turning serious.

Cassandra leaned forward and gave her friend a peck on the cheek.

"No, a proper one," Anna said moving forward and pressing her lips to those of her friend.

"Oh, that feels so nice," Cassandra said. "Your lips are so soft - kiss me again."

Anna leaned forward and kissed her friend, running her fingers through her friend's long, dark hair as she did it.

Brushing her fingers across Cassandra's face and neck, she took her hand in hers and brought it to her lips, gently kissing her fingers as she ran her hand up and down Cassandra's bare arms.

"You're such a tease," Cassandra said.

"Who says I'm teasing, babe?" Anna said, reaching forward and running her fingers down the soft skin beneath the open neck of Cassandra's unbuttoned shirt, the top few buttons of which were unfastened. "You like that?" she asked.

"You know I do," Cassandra sighed. Her body starting to shiver with excitement.

Chapter One

"Are you cold, babe?" Anna asked, noticing her friend trembling.

"No, just a little excited," Cassandra confessed, taking another drink from her glass of gin and tonic,

With all the buttons now undone, Anna leaned forward to give her friend a lingering kiss. Once again, Anna stroked Cassandra's bare arms, rising to her shoulders and neck and pulling her toward her so she could kiss her again. Gently, Anna moved her hands around Cassandra's neck and slid them down her back, pausing to teasingly twang the elastic strap of her bra.

"Oh, Mrs Waters, you certainly have a gentle touch," Cassandra breathlessly sighed.

"Thank you, Miss Wyvern," she replied.

Anna moved from her chair and kneeled between Cassandra's legs. Once again, she kissed her friend's full and passionate lips while gently trailing the back of her fingernails from Cassandra's neck, down her torso and on to her bare stomach. Then, back up, before pausing to gently caress her friend's breasts.

Chapter One

"Oh God, that feels so nice," Cassandra said, as Anna kissed her neck then, moved down to her breasts.

"You like that, beautiful lady?" she asked.

"Very much."

"How about this?" Anna said, flicking her tongue across Cassandra's erect nipples before taking one in her mouth and tenderly sucking it.

"Don't stop, please don't stop," Cassandra quietly gasped, running her fingers through Anna's hair before pulling off Anna's t-shirt and tossing it aside. "Kiss me again," Cassandra said, standing. Anna also rose and pressed her soft body against the body of her friend.

Cassandra put her arm around Anna's waist and tickled the small of her back before bringing them up Anna's back and, with one deft motion, unhooking her bra. That, too, fell to the floor.

"I think we'd better go inside," Anna said, suggestively widening her eyes. "There are things I want to do to you that we can't do out here."

Taking Cassandra by the hand, she led her into the house. As soon as they were inside, Anna fell to her knees and undid her friend's jeans. As they fell to the floor, Cassandra stepped out of

Chapter One

them. Drawing Cassandra close, Anna pressed her lips to the thin fabric of Cassandra's underwear and breathed in deeply then exhaling and letting the warmth of her breath penetrate the white cotton to the soft skin beneath.

Anna stroked Cassandra's legs, running her hand up and down them, pulling her close with her free hand.

"I think we'd better get you out of these," she said, sliding down Cassandra's underwear.

Again, Anna ran her hands up and down the outside of Cassandra's legs, relishing how soft the skin felt beneath her fingers. Then, moving her hands to the inside of Cassandra's legs, she slid them up her inner thighs before pausing to gently part Cassandra's lips.

"Oh God," said Cassandra. "That feels amazing."

Anna moved forward and flicked her tongue across her friend's lips, parting them with her slim fingers and giving her clitoris a lick.

"You'll smear your lipstick," Cassandra sighed.

Chapter One

"You're worth it, babe," Anna replied, her tongue darting back and forth as she began stroking Cassandra with practised fingers.

"My knees are trembling it feels so nice," Cassandra said. "Shall we lie down?"

"Whatever you want, babe," Anna said.

As Anna lay down, Cassandra kneeled next to Anna and undid her friend's slacks before pulling them down.

"Ooh, no underwear," Cassandra said with delight. "And so wet, too," she said, running her hand up her friend's leg, pausing to lightly touch Anna's swollen lips.

As the two naked women lay next to one another, they kissed and caressed one another's warm bodies that, now that the sun was bathing them in warm rays, began to glisten in the heat. With each woman gently teasing one another with a delicate, feminine touch it wasn't long before Anna's back began to arch, and her eyes close with pleasure.

"Oh God, I'm going to cum," she gasped. "Don't stop."

Chapter One

"I'm won't stop, I promise," Cassandra breathlessly whispered, as she also began to reach a peak of sexual ecstasy.

"I'm cumming," Anna said, said, her face showing the unmistakable signs of pleasure.

"Me too," Cassandra gasped, French-kissing her friend.

"That was amazing," Anna said, as the two lovers held each other, stroking each one another's soft skin, each trying to catch their breath as the waves of pleasure that had swept over them began to subside.

"I needed that," Cassandra said, tears filling her eyes. "There's more to life than sex, I know, but I don't even like him very much," Cassandra said, her mind wandering back to her problems at home. "He's not very bright, he's ill-mannered, and the things he likes bore me to tears. Why do grown men enjoy running around a wood pretending to shoot each other? They call it Airsoft but I call it pathetic! I want to have walks in the country, have long talks about books, art, music, and our future together. I want a knight in shining armour, not a tosser in tinfoil!" she laughed.

Chapter One

"So, what are you going to do about it?" Anna asked, stroking her friend's side, and gently kissing her.

"I don't know. The chance of meeting someone else while this lockdown is in place seem remote – and would I even want him, if I did? I'm getting pissed off being made to feel like a whore because I want more than two minutes of missionary position sex a couple of times a week. I swear he'd rather stuff his face than have sex with me. I want a man who when he sees me in the kitchen bends me over the kitchen table and tears my knickers off with his teeth before giving me a good seeing to, French-kissing me as he's cumming! I don't want a man who, when he sees me in the kitchen, clicks his fingers and tells me to hurry up with his dinner as he's meeting one of his dickhead friends to buy a new toy gun!"

"Sex in the kitchen can be great fun," laughed Anna. "Just last night Andy had me on the kitchen table, rubbing ice cubes on my nipples and licking my clitoris after cleaning his teeth. There must have been spearmint still in his mouth as it was … wow!" she enthused, her eyes glazing over at the memory.

Chapter One

"I have a very vivid imagination. For the right man, I'd be the woman he'd been looking for all his life," said Cassandra. "He seems to think it's alright for men to want filthy sex but if a woman is like that then they must be a slut as his 'Mother was never like that'."

"Oh my God, he never said that did he?"

"Yes, he bloody did! Despite lockdown, she still visits and I can see her looking around to see whether the cleaning has been done and the clothes put away. I even caught her running her fingers over the windowsill and then looking at them to see if they were dirty."

"Yikes", Anna said, drawing the corners of her mouth down in dismay.

"Now his father has got into genealogy and thinks the family may own some land in the Wye Valley."

"Ooh, nice," Anna replied.

"Yes, dickhead wants to go and look at it and wants me to go with him."

"That's good, no?" Anna said, stroking her friend's bare back.

"No. He only wants me there so that he can make sure I can't see you. I swear he wants me on

Chapter One

a short leash so that he can keep an eye on me," Cassandra said, leaning forward to kiss her friend on the mouth.

"See, I told you I wasn't worried about you smearing my lipstick," Anna laughed, as Cassandra leaned back on her elbow with her lips now smeared in Anna's lipstick. "Come here," Anna said, wiping the lipstick off Cassandra's face with her thumb.

"Thank you," Cassandra said.

"My pleasure, babe," Anna replied. "So, are you going to go with him tomorrow?"

"Well, it's a day out but I know it will end in an argument with him and him saying something nasty or comparing me to someone he'd seen online."

"I hate that," said Anna said in agreement. "We can't all be Kim Kardashian but then even Kim Kardashian isn't Kim Kardashian, the amount of work she's had done."

"God, I hate the twenty-first century. It's all pandemics, lockdowns, Facebook, and bullshit," Cassandra said, looking around for her drink and then remembering she'd left it in the garden.

Chapter One

"Yes, it seems geared to make people feel crap about their lives – hey, spend a little more money on crap you don't need and you, too, can lead the life of a millionaire z-lister!" Anna said, mocking the way adverts are geared to make what's being sold a necessity.

"I want to go back a hundred years and meet a real man. I want to be loved, cherished, and seduced. I want to know that when he looks at me that he feels lucky to have me and not thinking 'Oh, she'll do until something better comes along'."

"So, let's think what we can do to get you out of this rut, Cass. I was watching *The Witches of Eastwick* the other night, and they manifested their ideal man."

"Hang on, I don't want Jack Nicholson. Wasn't he supposed to be the devil in it? That said, I would love someone mystical and mysterious," Cassandra said, lost in thought as she looked through Ann's open patio doors and at the trees at the bottom of Anna's garden.

"Then try manifesting him," suggested Anna, stroking her friend's bare back.

Chapter One

"What do you mean?" asked Cassandra, Anna's suggestion rousing her from her reverie.

"Be clear about what you want and ask the universe to send it to you."

"That sounds like mumbo-jumbo to me," laughed Cassandra.

"What have you got to lose? If it doesn't work then you'll be no worse off than you are now. If it does work then you may have to buy yourself a more comfortable kitchen table!"

Both women laughed and fell silent before Cassandra sat up and looked around the room for her clothes.

"Write it down," Anna said, moving her hand as though she were writing before she also began to dress.

"Yes, I do know what the word means," laughed Cassandra. "Funnily enough, though, it was just what I was thinking. Have you got some paper and a pen?"

"Sure," Anna said, rising to her feet and walking back to her kitchen. Cassandra could hear her rummaging through a kitchen drawer before, a few moments later, returning with a pen and notepad. "Make it succinct, that way you can

Chapter One

repeat it to the universe as often as you remember."

"I want to be seduced," Cassandra said, saying the words as she wrote them down.

"That should do it," laughed Anna, blowing her friend a kiss. "So, are you going to go tomorrow?"

"Yes - it beats staring at four walls," Cassandra replied.

Now that they were both dressed, they finished their drinks.

"Well, I suppose I'd better get going," Cassandra said. "Thanks for the sex!"

"You're more than welcome, babe. I'd half-forgotten how good it feels to have a woman in my arms," Anna replied, kissing her index finger, then pressing her finger against Cassandra's lips. "You've still got a bit of my lipstick on your face," she added.

"Will you wipe it off for me?" Cassandra asked. "I don't want dickhead thinking I've been enjoying myself!"

With the evidence of their latest tryst removed, the two women said their goodbyes and Cassandra left as Anna stood in her doorway for a

Chapter One

moment to wave goodbye before closing the door once she had seen Cassandra closed the front gate and step out onto the pavement that ran alongside the road of the quiet cul-de-sac. With dread, she began the walk home.

"I want to seduced," she repeated to herself, repeating the phrase all the way home. "I want to be seduced, I want to be seduced," she murmured, as though it were a mantra. "I want to be seduced."

Chapter Two

The sun rose early next morning and with no cloud in the sky to mask its warming rays, those rays fell on the small Welsh town as its inhabitants awoke to the new day.

"Are you coming, or what?" Cassandra's partner, Simeon, asked.

"Yes. I'm sick of sitting here looking at these four walls," Cassandra replied.

Simeon let out a sigh and rolled his eyes before moving to a map his father had printed off for him the night before.

"Well, if you're not ready in ten minutes, then I'm going without you," he said.

"I'm ready now," Cassandra replied, biting her lip. Any argument now would cause Simeon to leave her at home for the day and a day out would be a welcome break, even it was only to enjoy the change of scenery.

Simeon sighed a second time and checked his pockets for his car keys.

"I need to concentrate today, so no whinging - please," he demanded, drawing out the final word so that it sounded sarcastic.

Soon, the pair were in his car and driving toward their destination in the Wye Valley.

Chapter Two

"It's beautiful here," Cassandra said, admiring the old houses and ancient ruins that sat amongst the verdant landscape. "Why haven't we come here before?"

"I have," Simeon replied.

"Yes, but I haven't."

"Ah well, you have now," Simeon said, making no attempt to hide the irritation in his voice.

He indicated right and drove his car across the small bridge that left Wales behind and entered England. Lost in thought, Cassandra was surprised when he parked and quickly turned off the car's engine.

"Is this it?" she asked.

"Is this what?"

"The place you said your father wanted you to visit."

"No, that will involve a bit of walking. Are you ready, fatty?" he asked as he leaned into the car, slamming the door without waiting for a reply.

The pair walked alongside the beautiful Wye, Cassandra admiring the view and Simeon texting his friends.

Chapter Two

"I feel like I've been here before," Cassandra said, mistakenly saying the words aloud.

"Yes, of course you do," Simeon replied, frowning as the words Cassandra had spoken jolted him from his messages.

"It can't be up here," Cassandra said, as Simeon pushed aside some brambles and began walking up an overgrown path, past stones and trees that were damp with moss.

"Do you want to read it!" Simon barked, pushing the map into Cassandra's chest.

"I was just saying," she responded.

"Well don't," came the brusque reply.

"It says it's a nature reserve."

"Did I not warn you not to start?" Simeon replied.

As the pair ascended the broken path, treading carefully and occasionally slipping on a knotted root or taking a small jump as their route crossed a small woodland stream, Simeon slipped.

"Oh, bollocks," he said, brushing the dirt from his jeans.

"Is that a house?" Cassandra asked, pointing at what appeared to be a chimney amongst the leaves and branches.

Chapter Two

"I wouldn't have thought so," came the terse response. "There are no lanes to it and the only path is the one that we've just walked. I'm knackered," he added.

The two of them walked a little nearer to what appeared to Cassandra to be a cottage. A dry-stone wall, common in the depths of even the densest of woodlands in the area, prevented a direct route. Simeon spied a gap, and what remained of an old wooden gate. Attempting to open it, it fell off its hinges and broke in two.

"It is a house," he conceded.

"See, you never believe me," Cassandra replied.

"Don't start," he remarked, giving her a look of contempt.

"Just saying."

"Well don't," he responded, drawing down the corners of his mouth in disgust before making his way to what appeared to be a curtain of ivy. "Hey, here's a door," he said, sounding the first note of enthusiasm he had sounded that day. "Let's see if there's anything worth nicking," he said aloud, laughing at the thought of such easy pickings.

Chapter Two

"Open!" Cassandra said with surprise, pointing at what appeared to be a shop sign behind the glass of the door.

"Don't know what that is," Simeon said as he turned the door's handle, the idea too challenging to think about as he pushed the door open. As soon as the door was wide enough, he entered; Cassandra followed him.

"It looks like some sort of shop," he said as he spied the counter, dusty shelves, and an ornate cash register. As the sunshine barely penetrated the dense foliage outside, he squinted into the gloom of the ancient room.

"Is it some sort of apothecary shop?" Cassandra asked. "There seem to be a lot of bottles and potions on those shelves."

"A what?" Simeon asked, betraying his ignorance, and making Cassandra wince.

"An apothecary – like a chemist or herbalist, but maybe with a few spells," she enthused.

"Let's see if there's anything worth taking," came the response.

Cassandra squinted about the darkened room before letting out a startled gasp as her gaze

Chapter Two

fell upon someone sat in the darkest corner, looking back at her.

"There's someone in here," she whispered to Simeone, taking a few steps backwards.

"Yes, of course there is," Simeon scoffed, filling his pocket with something he'd taken off a shelf.

"No, really – over there," she replied, looking at Simeon and gesturing with her thumb in the manner of a hitchhiker. She had only looked away for a second but when she looked back the figure had gone. Next to where it had sat, a heavy velvet curtain billowed, as though moved by a breeze.

"I warned you not to start," Simeon said, adding an impatient tut.

"No, really. He was there - gaunt, with wispy white hair and dressed in black."

"Are you sure it wasn't the butler from *The Rocky Horror Picture Show*?" Simeon asked facetiously, once again laughing at Cassandra.

"Actually, he looked very similar to him," Cassandra responded, not rising to Simeon's barb.

"Come on, let's go," Simeon said, stuffing the last of what he'd found that was worth

Chapter Two

stealing into his pockets. "I'll have to come back when I've got a torch. We'll be stumbling around like a pair of idiots if we look around the rest of the place, what with all that ivy over the windows."

"I don't need a light, I'm sure I've been here before," Cassandra replied.

"When was that then? An hour ago you were saying you'd never been to the Wye Valley! Then you said something about the river and now you've been here!"

"What did I ever see in you?" Cassandra said, her patience having finally snapped.

"I was wondering what I ever saw in you," he countered. "We have nothing common - except for sex."

"And that's crap," she hissed.

"What? The sex or that being all we have in common."

"Both," Cassandra hissed, her eyes flaming so brightly that even in the little light afforded by the open door, Simeon could tell her emotions were running high.

"Let's go," he said, taking a few short steps to the door, opening it wide before slamming it

Chapter Two

behind him leaving Cassandra alone inside the room and having to prise the door open for herself.

The walk back to the car was a silent one, as was their journey home.

"I'm sick of this," Cassandra thought to herself. "I want to be seduced – and seduced by someone that values me."

Chapter Three

The journey back home remained a silent one right back to the street in which they lived. When they pulled up outside their house, Simeon almost leapt from the car the moment the engine had stopped running; he then briskly walked to the house and after opening its door he entered and slammed it shut behind him, leaving Cassandra to search in her purse for her keys in order to open it.

"Well, that went well," Cassandra said to Simeon, as she entered the house and closed the door behind her.

"Pretty much as I expected," came the reply.

"So, what's the problem? If you hate being with me then why did you ask me to give up my place to move in with you?" she asked, taking off her jacket and tossing her long hair over her shoulders.

Simeon ran his fingers through his thinning hair, puffed out his cheeks, and pulled up his jogging bottoms.

"I figured you'd do until something better came along. I wasn't expecting a pandemic to

Chapter Three

scuttle that fucking plan and leave me stuck with you," he said.

"So, you had me give up my place and move in with you knowing you were going to end it when you got bored? You asshole!" Cassandra said, shouting, and pointing her finger at Simeon in rage.

"Yes - it was just sex and I figured as soon as I got bored with shagging you, I'd move on to something better," Simeon said, his face breaking into a grin as he folded his arms and waited for her reply.

"So, you just wanted me for sex?"

"Yes. I hadn't realised that even that would be crap. I need a woman that likes sex, not someone frigid – like you."

"Frigid? You have no idea! I am a very passionate woman. Ever thought that given you're such a selfish asshole out of bed that you're also a selfish asshole in bed?" Cassandra said, moving to the kitchen to put away some dishes she had left on the draining board. Shaking with rage, she dropped a plate and it shattered on the hard kitchen floor.

Chapter Three

"I'm great in bed – if I find the woman I'm screwing attractive. No man wants to spend half an hour on foreplay just to have someone whinge that they didn't have an orgasm. You don't understand men if you think any of them will put up with that," he said, kicking the broken fragments of china across the floor.

"So, you don't even find me attractive? You're hardly Johnny Depp yourself! Do you think any woman is dying to have you sweating away on top of her for two minutes a few times a week?" Cassandra said, pointing at Simeon's stomach.

"You saying I'm fat? It didn't seem to bother you when we got together. I thought you'd be grateful of finding anyone the way you act," he shouted, unfolding his arms before slapping away her hand, taking a step forward and pointing a finger into her face.

"Don't try and intimidate me, you bastard – I'll stick a knife in you," she said, picking up a knife from the draining board and pointing it at her aggressor, the wild look in her eye causing Simeon to take a step backwards.

Chapter Three

"Look, we got together without even knowing each other," he began, taking a second step backwards, then pacing the room and trying to add emphasis to his words with flailing hand gestures.

"And now I know it was just so you could drain your balls a few times a week," Cassandra hissed.

Simeon stopped pacing up and down in front of Cassandra before smiling and nodding in agreement.

Cassandra pursed her lips, closed her eyes, and shook her head in disgust.

"You don't understand women at all, do you? I'm uninhibited but I need to feel needed, wanted, attractive, and desired – and loved."

"Yeah, well good luck with that," he scoffed. "And uninhibited! You freaked when I tried to stick it in your ass the other night."

"You don't do something like that without even asking! Everyone has their likes and dislikes and to just assume you can do what you want when you want is taking the piss," she seethed, running her hand through her hair and tying it into a ponytail. "So, where do we go from here?"

Chapter Three

"I don't know. Tinder? Plenty of Fish?" said Simeon, smirking.

"You seem to forget that there's a pandemic," Cassandra replied, causing the smirk to drop from his face.

"No, I didn't - it's the only reason you're still here," he said, reminding Cassandra that she had been little more than a stop-gap for him.

"Well, make the most of it as I won't be here much longer," Cassandra said with confident resignation. "You're a slob and I deserve better."

"And you're a frigid nutcase that doesn't know a good thing when she sees it," came the hostile rebuke. "I'm off on the Xbox," he added, leaving the kitchen, and walking a few paces to the living room.

Cassandra put the rest of the dishes away, then went to their bedroom. A few hours later she heard Simeon's footsteps on the stairs.

"Fancy a shag?" he asked, as though the events of just a few hours earlier had never happened.

"Yes, I'd love one," Cassandra said, as Simeon smiled and began unbuttoning his jeans.

"Great," he said.

Chapter Three

"Just not with you," she added.

"You bitch," he hissed through gritted teeth, leaving the room, and returning to his Xbox in the living room downstairs.

Cassandra walked to the airing cupboard in the spare room and removed a duvet.

"Ah, I knew you were joking," Simeon said, having suddenly appeared in the doorway behind her. "I'm the bomb."

"Yes, but with a three-inch fuse," Cassandra replied, pointing at his groin before brushing past him and descending the stairs for a night on the sofa.

Chapter Four

The next morning, Cassandra awoke from a fitful night's sleep. Making her way to the bathroom, she took a shower. Knowing what Simeon really felt about her and how he must have felt when he'd had sex with her made her feel so dirty that she tried her best to wash every trace of him off her. All night long she had dreamt of the figure she had seen in the apothecary shop the previous day. She had felt a strange sense of déjà vu as Simeon had driven through the Wye Valley. Then, when they had crossed the little bridge leaving Wales behind and entering England, it seemed as though imagination and memory had merged; like seeing the face of an old friend who, while still being someone she recognised, had suffered much by the march of time.

"I want to be seduced," she told herself as she dried herself, remembering the imprecation to the universe that her friend Anna had suggested she repeat.

After breakfast, she washed her bowl and picked up her car keys. Something seemed to be pulling her back to the place she had visited the previous day.

Chapter Four

Cassandra closed the front door behind her and made her way to her car. What was the force compelling her to make the return journey alone, she wondered?

As she passed the nearby racecourse and entered the snaking lanes in front of her, she began to feel unburdened, as though the recent memories of life with Simeon were falling from her grasp like the loose pages of an old book.

As she crossed the bridge from Wales into England what felt like memories, but which she told herself must be her imagination, blew away the cobwebs of her despair and frustration.

She drove past the old pub and parked on the hill that led out of the village.

"My God, this is such a beautiful place," she said to herself as she parked. After locking her car, she walked back down the hill and then onto the path that ran alongside the silently flowing river that she had walked alongside the previous day. To her right, a few old houses and cottages were embracing the morning sun; to her left, the river and, beyond that, old woodland that stretched away from her with such beauty it left her spellbound.

Chapter Four

A cold chill ran through her as she passed the old stone boathouse, as though the pleasant memories she had felt a little while before had been replaced by something terrifying.

Silently, she made her way to the overgrown path, pushing aside brambles and nettles and then on into the woodland. Above her, a verdant canopy; below her knotted tree roots and broken stones, rising in front of her as though the woodland welcomed her with outstretched arms.

"Ah, no people," she whispered, as sunbeams penetrated the leaves and kissed her pretty, smiling face. Only the sound of birdsong and the gentle breeze through those leaves gave a voice to nature.

Had it really been such a steep climb the day before? Narrow and, at times, slippery she continued her climb. Thoughts of Tolkien's tales flashed across her mind. Just when she thought that she must have taken a wrong path and that no house could be in such an inaccessible place, let alone a shop, she saw its chimney and the dry-stone wall that surrounded what must once have been a garden.

Chapter Four

She stepped over the remains of the gate that Simeon had broken in two the day before and entered. If there hadn't been a chimney breaking free from the clutches of ivy that sought to hold it in its grasp, ivy that hung in a thick cascade around the property, one might be forgiven for not even realising that a house lay beneath the jade blanket.

Taking a few steps forward she found the door through which Simeon and she had entered the previous day.

The room was just as dark as the day before, lit only by the narrowest shafts of sunlight that pierced the ivy hanging about the windows.

"I've been expecting you," came a voice, causing Cassandra to jump.

"I'm sorry - the sign on the door said that you were open," Cassandra said, apologetically, pointing at the sign that hung on the door.

"Indeed, I am - it's just been a very long time since I had a customer," the voice replied, again causing Cassandra to start as this time its owner had silently moved behind her. Then, an unseen hand closed the door.

Chapter Four

"It's very dark in here," Cassandra said, as she began feeling that her return to the shop had not been such a good idea.

"I shall light a lamp for you," said the apothecary, lighting an old oil lamp that resided on the edge of one of the shop counters.

The light was soft and just bright enough to show Cassandra the same gaunt and withered features she had seen the day before. His frock coat and trousers, at one time, must have been black but now decades of dust had turned them grey.

"Why were you expecting me?" Cassandra asked, her heart fluttering like a bird in a gilded cage.

"You don't remember?"

"Remember? Yesterday? Yesterday was my first visit," Cassandra replied, her forehead creasing into a perplexed frown.

"Then you don't remember," the man observed, letting out a sigh.

"No - anyway, I'm Cassandra Wyvern. You are?" she asked.

"Lucius - Lucius d'Orleans," Lucius offered, extending a hand.

Chapter Four

"French? I thought you had an accent," Cassandra responded, trying to sound upbeat even though she now felt a little panic-stricken.

"Yes, I am French - despite the centuries I've been here, I still have an accent," Lucius replied. "I think it's because I haven't fraternised very much with the locals – I'm not the most sociable of people. When you spend fifty years without talking to a soul you forget the local vernacular."

"Centuries?" Cassandra queried, but not wishing to press the matter when she didn't receive a reply.

Cassandra gazed around the dusty, darkened room and tried to imagine how it must have once looked. Antique bottles full of powder and potions sat on shelves whilst a large wooden counter sat in front of three of the walls; the back counter had a large and ornate till on it.

"That was a very inciteful description that you gave of an apothecary yesterday," Lucius said. "Not all of us cast spells, of course - or practise the art of divination."

Cassandra looked at Lucius and even in the twilight world in which they stood, she noticed

Chapter Four

the sapphire blue of his eyes shining bright on his lined an aged face.

"Divination? I'd love to know my future," Cassandra said with excitement.

"Then step this way," Lucius replied, walking toward the back wall, and sweeping aside the heavy velvet curtain that Cassandra had seen moving the day before. "Please, sit down," Lucius said, pulling an old chair away from a large, dark table that formed the centrepiece of the room, for his guest.

"I'm a bit nervous," Cassandra said, trying to make herself comfortable, as Lucius walked to a bureau and took from it a deck of tarot cards.

"These are rather special," he said. "They were produced by my friend Jean Noblet in Marseille in the year sixteen-fifty."

Returning to the table, he placed the cards down and dragged a chair across well-worn floorboards before sitting in it, opposite Cassandra.

"What happens now?" Cassandra asked as Lucius moved the oil lamp that he had brought with them from the room in which they had met.

Chapter Four

Cassandra felt a little shocked to see Lucius leaning toward her.

"What are you doing?" she asked, letting out a fearful gasp.

"Shuffle the pack and then give them to me," he said, tapping the cards with his index finger.

Cassandra picked up the pack and gave them a shuffle but because nerves were now getting the better of her, she dropped them.

"It's alright, don't be nervous. Please, try again," Lucius said.

Cassandra shuffled the cards a second time and then handed them to Lucius who proceeded to spread them face down on the table.

"Pick three," he said, his piercing eyes staring at Cassandra as she looked at the cards. Picking three, she pulled them away from the rest of the pack.

"Right," said Lucius, turning over the first card. "Ah, *Le Pendu*," he said. "Sorry, the Hanged Man."

"Not good?" Cassandra asked, thinking the card must be a bad omen.

Chapter Four

"Maybe, maybe not. It would suggest that you're feeling trapped, and stuck in a situation that is making you unhappy. But," he continued, "do you notice the halo around his head? That suggests that with thoughtful actions you can change things."

"I think I know what that means," Cassandra enthused. "It's very accurate."

"Please, turn over the next card," Lucius said.

A second after he had spoken the words Cassandra turned over the cards and let out a fearful sigh.

"Ah, *La Mort.* Sorry, Death," Lucius said, scratching the side of his face and looking at Cassandra for a reaction.

"Oh no, not more misery - I've had just about as much as I can take," Cassandra said, her voice beginning to quake with emotion.

"No, it can be a very positive card," Lucius said, reaching across the table and giving Cassandra's hand a gentle squeeze. "It means death of an old chapter in your life, and the beginning of a new one - major changes may be coming your way."

Chapter Four

"Thank God for that," Cassandra said, wiping a tear from her cheek. It wasn't what the cards had predicted that brought forth a tear but the fact that it had been such a long time since anyone had held her hand and that simple act of kindness had touched her.

"Would you like to turn over the last card?" Lucius said, smiling at Cassandra.

"Yes," she whispered, turning over the last card.

"Ah, *L'Amoureux*," Lucius said. "The Lover."

"What does that card mean?" Cassandra asked.

"Well," Lucius began. "If you're in a relationship, it could mean that there will be a rekindling of love and romance."

"I can't see that happening," Cassandra laughed, running her free hand through her hair.

"It signifies a very intense bond between two people that goes beyond infatuation. This card represents a deep and intense attraction," Lucius said, pausing for breath. "Passion, romance, and understanding."

"Really? That sounds perfect – amazing," Cassandra enthused.

Chapter Four

"I'm glad that they were all so positive for you," Lucius said.

"The sooner the better," Cassandra replied. "I don't want any more flings. All my friends have found someone - what's wrong with me?"

Cassandra had meant it as a rhetorical question so was not expecting an answer.

"Nothing - you're beautiful," Lucius replied.

"No-one has ever said that to me," Cassandra said, feeling both embarrassed and tearful.

"Yes, they have – I said it to you. I said it just then, and I said it to you a century or two ago," Lucius replied

"I need to think about all this," Cassandra said, feeling so confused that her mind began to spin. "I don't know what you mean when you said it to me a century or two ago."

"You don't remember?" Lucius asked.

"I remember something but I don't know what," Cassandra replied. "They feel liked fragments of a dream."

"I'm sure it will all come back to you – in time," Lucius said, reaching out for the cards and putting them in a neat pile.

Chapter Four

"I'm confused," Cassandra said, biting her lip as though she were puzzling over something. You know when you visit somewhere new or meet someone for the first time and it feels like you've either been there before or met them before?

"Yes, I know that feeling very well," Lucius said, giving Cassandra a smile.

"Well, that's how I feel – and I can't believe I'm telling you that, given we've only just met."

"No, we've not just met. We've known each other over a few lifetimes," Lucius said.

"Yes, that's what it also feels like to me. It's not a feeling I've ever had before."

"Is it a nice feeling?" Lucius asked.

"It was terrifying down by the boathouse but now that I'm here, it feels like nothing I've ever felt."

"As though dust and dirt are turning to gold?" Lucius asked.

"Yes, I suppose so," Cassandra replied, feeling a little uncertain.

Lucius swept his hand across a dusty shelf on a wall to his left. Pouring the dust he had gathered from his left hand into his right hand, he

Chapter Four

threw the dust in the air. Cassandra sat in awe as the tiny particles turned to gold and lightly fell on the table in front of her, shimmering in the light of the lamp.

"That's amazing!" she said. "I really need time to think about this - but I will say this, Lucius," she added.

"What's that?" Lucius asked, his curiosity piqued.

"You're amazing!"

"Thank you, Cassandra. I was hoping you'd still feel the same way about me as I feel about you."

"Lucius, I need time to think," Cassandra said, looking up at the ceiling as though seeking divine inspiration.

"Of course - please, do whatever makes you happy," Lucius said, again reaching across the table to tenderly touch Cassandra's hand.

"I must go," Cassandra said, reluctantly removing her hand from the warm-hearted embrace with which Lucius held it.

"Well, you know where I am," he said, walking with Cassandra to the shop's door.

Chapter Four

"Yes, you've been very kind," she replied. "I shan't forget it."

Cassandra made her way back down the narrow woodland path, pushing aside the brambles and nettles that blocked her way. Then, once again, she found herself on the banks of the beautiful river. Lost in a reverie of what had just happened at the cottage, what her fortune had told her, and the kindness Lucius had shown her, the half an hour it took her to walk back to her car seemed to pass by in just a few minutes.

Back at the house that she shared with Simeon, she expected an argument and an interrogation over where she had been. Instead, she found a note.

"Gone to Paul's for a few days. Hope you're gone by the time I get back. Stick your keys through the letterbox. Hatefully yours, Simeon," Cassandra read, whispering the words to herself.

Cassandra screwed up the note before having second thoughts and unfurling it. Walking to her oven she switched on a gas ring and set it alight.

"Screw you, asshole," she muttered, as it turned to ashes.

Chapter Five

That night, Cassandra spent a second night on the sofa, despite Simeon not being home and the bed they had once shared lying empty. All night she thought of what her cards had said – and the man that had interpreted them. What was it about him that felt so familiar? She had never had a feeling of déjà vu about a person but when he had held her hand it felt as though it had reawakened a long-forgotten memory, yet try as she might she could not remember where or when they had ever met. Then there were those eyes! The white hair might have been thin and wispy, his skin that of an old man, yet his eyes seemed to be a doorway to her past.

She arose early that morning, showered, made herself breakfast and made up her mind to return to the shop deep within the woodland of the Wye Valley. The wretched lockdown was still in place, so she knew that any unnecessary travel was forbidden but this journey felt to be a journey that she needed to take if only to speak to Lucius, and to ask him how she might know him and where before they had met. He may not have the answers but the alternative was to stay within the four walls that were no longer those of a home but

Chapter Five

those of a house, all the while waiting for the sound of a key in the front door that would tell her that her ex, Simeon, had returned. Then she paused: in thinking of such things, she had said the word 'ex', rather than sully her mind or lips with his name.

The drive into the Wye Valley felt strangely familiar but not the familiarity one might have of a recent memory but the memory one has of a first embrace, kiss, or homecoming. She sighed with pleasure as she realised that it felt safe and softly secure, something she had missed.

As she arrived at what should have been the turning to the village she had visited the day before, its bridge had gone. Strange, she thought, as she parked her car on the Welsh side of the valley. Within a few minutes, she had found and descended some steps and walked to the water's edge. There, a small craft was ferrying a few passengers across the small expanse of water. Patiently, she waited her turn, feeling uncomfortable that the locals not only appeared to be dressed in clothes of a bygone age but that her clothes seemed to be a cause of concern and alarm to them.

Chapter Five

As she reached England, she couldn't help but notice that the tarmac road with double-yellow lines that she had seen the day before had gone and been replaced by one made of cobblestones. A horse and cart passed her, then another.

"Well, it is a rural village. Maybe it's a quaint tradition," she told herself, remembering her days at university and reading of the May Day traditions in Gloucestershire and the Forest of Dean that often involved Morris Dancers.

Hadn't the old pub been named something different when she had passed it the day before? As she began walking alongside the river, two women walked towards her, both dressed in garb that to Cassandra looked more than a century out-of-date. Both women looked at Cassandra in mute astonishment. She glanced back to her car on the far banks and spied a small group of people standing beside it, pointing at it as if it had been an Italian Supercar.

"Haven't they ever seen a car before!" she said to herself.

Walking alongside the river, again the old boathouse made her shudder as she passed it.

Chapter Five

Then she looked at it again – old? It now appeared considerably less old than it had the day before.

Cassandra looked for the overgrown entrance to the path but it appeared as if someone had removed the brambles, nettles, and ferns since the previous day and she now had no trouble finding the route that led to the old steps.

The path was as broken and precipitous as she remembered, with every footfall a gamble as to whether the damp moss that covered the stones would send her tumbling. Onwards she walked, again thinking about how the journey from the river to the shop seemed longer and steeper than she remembered. With eyes downcast to ensure each step was a safe one, she came to a sudden stop. When she raised her eyes in anticipation of seeing the thick curtain of ivy that had yesterday covered the house, today all the ivy had gone.

Cassandra pressed on, now feeling a little unsure as to whether she had somehow taken the wrong path. Had the path forked and she, watching where she carefully trod, taken a wrong turn and somehow lost her way?

The young woman came to an abrupt stop when she saw the little gate that had, just a few

Chapter Five

days before, fallen off its hinges and broken in two as Simeon had touched it. Now it appeared new.

"What's going on!" she said aloud, deciding that the only way to find an answer to such a question was to enter the apothecary shop and see if its proprietor was Lucius d'Orleans, the man that had such an effect on her the previous day.

"There's the 'open' sign, so it's definitely a shop of some sort," she told herself.

With some trepidation, she opened the door and was astonished to see every counter, cabinet, jar, and bottle gleaming.

"Hello," came a voice to her right. Quickly, Cassandra turned and saw a man she guessed to be around the same age as her. Perhaps Lucius had a son, she thought, given his eyes were the same colour of brilliant blue; but gone were the wrinkles and white wisps of hair, replaced by taut skin and black hair.

"I'm sorry, I was looking for Lucius d'Orleans," Cassandra said.

"I am he," the man said, smiling and extending a hand.

"I'm confused. I don't understand what's going on – it's as if I've stepped back in time. What

Chapter Five

year is this? When I left it was twenty twenty-one," Cassandra said in bewilderment.

"This is eighteen ninety-one," Lucius replied.

"Eighteen ninety-one! Is this for real?" Cassandra stammered, rubbing her face with her hand, and looking around the shop for something familiar.

"Yes, this is eighteen ninety-one. What year was it when you visited yesterday?" Lucius asked.

"That was also twenty twenty-one. Are all those people I saw half an hour ago living one hundred and thirty years ago?"

"No, they're living now. Every moment in time is happening right now. Ghosts aren't the spirits of the dead but a moment, or two, in time that has somehow availed itself to us. Of course, people die ..."

"So why aren't those people dead?" Cassandra interrupted.

"They are in twenty twenty-one but you're in eighteen ninety-one. You've somehow stepped from what we think of as the future into what we think of as the past," Lucius said. "Our concept of time is an illusion and is nothing more than our

Chapter Five

memories - everything that has ever been and ever will be is happening right now. The only reason we feel like we have a past is because our brain contains memories."

"And you? I spoke to you yesterday when you were old and yet today you are young. That means you must have been one hundred and sixty when I saw you yesterday!"

"Far older than that," Lucius said.

"Older? So why are you young-looking today if you're even older than one hundred and sixty?"

"Because yesterday I had nothing to live for and today I have you," Lucius said, closing the door. "Even now – in eighteen ninety-one – I have been waiting almost a hundred years for you to return to me. When we met yesterday, it was almost two-hundred and fifty years since we first met - and my loneliness had become unbearable."

"Hold on, you're going to have to explain a few things as that seems crazy. I do feel something strange about this place – about you, but I don't know what. It feels like déjà vu."

"I am French. I came over here with the Normans in the eleventh century. I was a member

Chapter Five

of the *Rose-Croix*. People think that Brotherhood only began in the seventeenth century but it was built on the esoteric truths of an ancient past. We discovered the secret of everlasting life."

"The *Rose-Croix*?" queried Cassandra,

"Yes - they're more often known as the Rosicrucians," Lucius said, looking intently at Cassandra for a reaction. "You're looking as if you've not heard of them."

"No, I haven't. Who are they?" Cassandra replied, the wheels of her mind turning as she sought to remember where she had heard the name.

"Lord Lytton wrote of us in *Zanoni* and Shelley in *St. Irvyne the Rosicrucian*," Lucius said. "Legend has it that we've been in existence since the sixteenth century and a popular theory is that our name was derived from our supposed founder, Christian Rosenkreuze, but I don't believe that such a man ever existed.

"In the popular imagination, it is believed that we originated in Germany, in the early seventeenth century, in the town of Cassell. An anonymous pamphlet was published that was supposed to be a message to professors of magic

Chapter Five

and mysticism that urged all men of science to band together as the writer was concerned about the moral welfare of the world and thought that a synthesis of all the arts and science could return mankind to a state of perfection. This, the writer imagined, could only be achieved with the assistance of the illuminated Brotherhood – the children of light who had been initiated into the mysteries of the Grand Orient.

"The writer stated that the head of our movement was someone known as 'C.R.C', a magician of the highest rank. At the age of fifteen, it was written that he undertook an arduous journey to Damascus, arriving at an unknown Arabian city named Damcar where he obtained arcane knowledge from a secret circle of theosophists who were all experts in the magical arts. There, the magi informed him that they had long been expecting him and related to him passages of his past life. After three years of instruction in the occult arts, he travelled to Egypt and onto the city of Fez. It was there that other masters taught him how to invoke the elemental spirits. After a few more years of study, he travelled to Spain, to both learn and to speak to

Chapter Five

the professors of that county. Scholars from that country derided him and told him that the principles and practice he had learned must have been taught to him by Satan. Other countries treated him in the same manner, and so he returned to Germany where he became a hermit."

"Is that why you're also a hermit?" Cassandra asked, causing Lucius to smile. "Sorry, I wasn't being facetious," she added.

"Back in Germany, he perfected the transmutation of base metals into gold and the elixir of life. The assistants that he had gathered about him became the basis of the Rosicrucian fraternity. In time, 'C.R.C' died, and for over a century his burial place was a secret. It was only a later generation of adepts that found his tomb while rebuilding one of his secret dwellings. His body was found in a state of perfect preservation, and many marvels were found buried alongside him, marvels that convinced the Brotherhood that they had a duty to make their secrets known to the world.

"Another year passed, and the *Confession of the Rosicrucian Fraternity* was published, addressed to the learned of Europe. Applications

Chapter Five

to join the Brotherhood, however, were ignored and by sixteen-twenty, the Brotherhood had all but disappeared.

"The published pamphlets leave the reader in no doubt that the Rosicrucians believed in the same alchemy, astrology, and occult forces of nature as Paracelsus. It is also stated that we believe that man contains the potentialities of the whole universe," Lucius said, all the while remaining motionless and silhouetted, his back against the shop door.

"But you said that none of that history goes back beyond the sixteenth century," Cassandra said. "Yet you also said you first came to this country in the eleventh century."

"Yes, I did - all those histories allude to an ancient Brotherhood that was far older than the Brotherhood of the sixteenth century," Lucius said, giving Cassandra an inscrutable smile.

"So, where and when did we first meet?" Cassandra asked.

"Six hundred years later was the first time we met and became lovers," Lucius said, smiling at the memory. "You meant everything to me, and a day with you meant more to me than the six-

Chapter Five

hundred years that had preceded them, years I had spent alone. Sadly, the French Revolution parted us as we had cause to visit the country in seventeen eighty-nine. We were viewed with suspicion by the *Montagnards,* revolutionaries led by Robespierre, Danton, and Marat, and were shot trying to flee the county in seventeen ninety-two - before I could impart to you the *Rose-Croix* secret of eternal life."

"So, where did we meet? Here, or France?" Cassandra asked.

"In the eighteenth century?" queried Lucius. "Yes."

"Oh, we met in Paris."

"How did we meet?" asked Cassandra.

"You were a courtesan. I wasn't a client of yours but I used to see you in the gin palaces of Montmartre and thought you were the most beautiful woman I had ever seen."

"I was a prostitute!" Cassandra said in astonishment, looking for a seat but finding none and leaning against one of the shop's counters.

"Yes, and it broke my heart to see you being used and abused by those unworthy of you. One

Chapter Five

night we chatted and took a walk by the banks of the Seine - it was there that I first kissed you."

"That sounds incredibly romantic," Cassandra said.

"Yes, ours was a passion that I had never known, nor ever imagined. I suppose the intervening years took their toll on me but just a few years ago you returned to me. Again, we became lovers, despite you being married. Ours was a passion like no other and threatened to consume us both. Then, just a few months ago your husband found out and killed you."

"What! Where?" Cassandra asked, hardly able to believe what she had heard, or that she had once been murdered.

"He hit you with a rock and threw you in the river, by the boathouse, down there," Lucius said, gesturing with an outstretched arm and pointed finger at where he imagined the boathouse might be, near the river Cassandra had walked past several times over the past few days.

Lucius looked at Cassandra, awaiting her reaction.

"And did she look like me?" she asked.

"Yes," Lucius replied.

Chapter Five

"That explains why those women were staring at me," Cassandra said, the moment of elucidation causing her to raise her voice.

"They must have thought you were a ghost," Lucius said.

"This is very strange and difficult for me," Cassandra said, looking around the room to distract herself, before walking to the glass jars that lined the walls.

"Yes, I'm sure it's very difficult to be here, but you've found your home. You've returned to me." Lucius said, pausing a moment. "Your immortal spirit has found me."

Cassandra felt a warm glow on hearing the words but feared turning, lest her expression betrayed her thoughts.

"You're a very seductive man, Lucius," she said.

"Thank you – and you're a very seductive woman."

"Bergamot, lemon oil, lavender oil," she said, running her hand across the mysterious bottles and reading their labels, labels which the day before had looked like faded parchment but which now looked new.

Chapter Five

"Yes, do you like perfumes? Here, I have a perfume for you – a bottle of *Hammam Bouquet* by Penhaligon. It has lavender, bergamot, Bulgarian rose, orris root, jasmine, cedar, sandalwood, amber and musk. It was made for men but is too feminine for a twenty-first-century taste. What with the scent of old books, powdered resins, and ancient rooms I thought of you," Lucius said, lifting a small bottle from beneath the shop counter.

"That's so kind of you, thank you. How did you know I'd return?" Cassandra asked, looking at Lucius over her shoulder and feeling a little embarrassed and unworthy that he had bought her a gift.

"You forgot the tarot?" he asked. "I know the future as well as the past for, as I said, every moment in time is happening right now."

"Jasmine, orange blossom, rose, violet," Cassandra continued, the magic of the bottles having cast their spell over her.

"Here, let me put a little on you," Lucius said. Cassandra hadn't heard his approach so was a little startled to hear him speak the words while standing so close to her. "May I?" he asked.

Chapter Five

"Of course," Cassandra said, in joyful abandon.

Standing behind Cassandra, Lucius swept aside Cassandra's hair, exposing her delicate neck. Dabbing the stopper of the bottle on her bare skin, he closed his eyes in ecstasy as both the perfume and scent of Cassandra left him feeling intoxicated.

"But why do you make such beautiful perfumes if you never have a customer?" Cassandra asked.

"I want to give the world beautiful things," he said. "Just because no one buys them, it doesn't devalue them. I must do something with my time and rather than destroy, I create – and what better things are there to create than something that is beautiful? Think of the author writing beautiful books that no-one will read – his words are no less beautiful because they're unread."

"Kiss me," Cassandra said, turning so that her eyelashes brushed his face. Looking up, her lips met with his. Lucius' fingers entwined with those of Cassandra. Then, letting go, he reached an arm around her waist and drew her close to him.

Chapter Five

"I won't let you get away so easily this time," he said.

"I have a lot to think about but I will be back – I promise," Cassandra said. "I must go, but I shall return."

With that, Cassandra left the shop and made her way back to her car. How long had she been in that embrace, she wondered, as it was now getting dark; a twilight sun already penetrated the verdant canopy above her.

Cassandra made her way back to the ferry and again felt uneasy at the silent trepidation with which the ferryman spied her. Shades of a setting sun were now caressing the village. Stepping back into Wales, she was relieved to find that her car was no longer eliciting the same curiosity that it had earlier that day. Driving away from the little town, she glanced in her rear-view mirror not quite believing that she was leaving a village - and time - a century before she'd been born.

The drive back to the house she shared with Simeon, and the thought of seeing him again wasn't something that caused her anxiety as she assumed the house would be empty; it was only when she drove into the street in which the house

Chapter Five

sat that she noticed that there was a light on in its living room, the tell-tale flickering suggesting it was either a TV or computer game. Only then did her anxiety cause her stomach to tie itself into twisted knots: Simeon had returned.

Chapter Six

Cassandra placed her key inside the front door's lock and turned it. Breathing heavily with anxious fear, she pushed the door open and entered before closing it quietly behind her

"What are you doing back?" Simeon asked. He had heard the key in the lock over the sound of his computer games and now stood leaning against the door frame of the door that entered the living room.

"I won't be staying," Cassandra replied.

"Eh? But you've got nowhere else to go."

"You said in that note that you wanted me to leave, so I'm leaving."

"What note? I didn't write any note." This wasn't the first time Simeon had done something and then denied having done it in the hope of having Cassandra doubt her sanity.

"Don't try and gaslight me, Sunshine! I burnt it," she responded.

"And what am I supposed to have said in this note?" Simeon asked, trying his best to sound both incredulous and exasperated.

"That you wanted me to leave - so I'm leaving,"

Chapter Six

"But you've nowhere to go," Simeon replied, his voice betraying his fear that his attempt at gaslighting Cassandra had this time failed.

"That's what you wanted, wasn't it! Separate me from my friends and family, have me give up my home and job, then I'm utterly dependent on you," Cassandra said, pushing past Simeon and making her way to the kitchen. Simeon having now moved from the doorway, attempted to hinder Cassandra's access to the kitchen.

"Friends? Those slags! Why do you want to hang around with them? If the pubs were still open they'd be dragging you out, telling you that you can do better than me - and getting you to act like them." Simeon said, raising his hand and pointing at Cassandra to enforce his point.

"No, they wouldn't - and even if I did meet up with them do you really think that I'm so easily led that I'd do what they said? That's you and your insecurities - if you felt better about yourself then you wouldn't feel so paranoid and imagine that I'm dreaming-up ways of leaving you! Well, this time I am."

"To go where? You've met someone else, haven't you? I knew it! Fucking women, I'm

Chapter Six

pissed off with all of them – they're all unfaithful, looking for someone with more money or a bigger car."

"I have not cheated on you, you ended it! Remember? It hasn't been working for months and knowing you were only waiting for something better was the final straw. I'm not a fucking doormat – I deserve to be more than someone's fuck buddy! I deserve to be loved and cherished and even if you changed, I don't want to be loved and cherished by you," Cassandra shouted, her eyes blazing in fury.

"Who is he?" Simeon asked, taking a step forward and trying to look threatening.

"You ended it! I've been back to the shop we visited and the spoken to the man there …" Cassandra began before being interrupted by Simeon.

"That old bastard behind the counter?" Simeon scoffed.

"I thought you hadn't seen him?"

"I didn't see him - I just remember you saying he looked like the butler from that crap film you like."

Chapter Six

"I thought you never believed anything I said," Cassandra said, pushing past Simeon and making her way to the bottom of the stairs.

"I don't, but you must have met someone. Women like you can't ever go it alone and always have to have a bloke in tow to pay their bills."

"Bullshit! I don't need a man for *anything*. I want to feel loved and cherished – everyone needs someone to make them feel special. You just made me feel like a stop-gap, someone to be used, abused, and tossed aside," Cassandra shouted, pointing her finger at Simeon who took it as his cue to again try to intimidate Cassandra by taking a step closer and puffing up his chest.

"You can't leave me," he said.

"Why? Because you're so kind? Because you make me feel so special? You didn't treat me nicely when you had the chance and now that I'm going, you're acting like a child that's had his toys taken off him."

"You bitch," he shouted.

"Come on, Si," came a man's voice from the living room. "I thought we were playing a game."

"Who's that?" Cassandra asked, shocked to realise that they were not alone.

Chapter Six

"Just a few of the lads," Simeon replied. "I'll be there now," he shouted, turning his head toward the living room.

"I'm going to get a few things and then I'll be gone," Cassandra said. "I've had enough of twenty twenty-one and this pandemic – and had enough of you. I'm going back to a different time and place."

"What the fuck are you talking about?" Simeon asked, drawing the corners of his mouth down, into a disgusted sneer.

"Today, I visited eighteen ninety-one, and that's where I'm going," Cassandra said, hissing the words with contempt before Simeon burst out laughing.

"You're a nutcase! Any man that wants you must be crazy."

"Well, that's my problem, isn't it!" Cassandra said as she ascended the stairs.

"What have I done that's so wrong? This is how men are," Simeon said, following her.

"No, they're not. You and your cretinous friends might be like it but there are men out there that love the things I love - and know that they

Chapter Six

have to treat a person they love with kindness as the thought of losing them is unbearable."

"You don't know men if that's what you think!" Simeon said with derision. "All we want is food on the table, a roof over our head, and a whore in the bedroom."

"Well, good luck finding the woman of your dreams. I'm sure you'll be very happy together," Cassandra said, turning her back on Simeon.

Suddenly, Simeon grabbed her hair and tried to pull her back down the stairs. Somehow, Cassandra freed herself and quickly turned.

"Don't hit me, you bastard," she said, taking a step backwards.

"How else are you going to learn?" Simeon said. Only now could Cassandra smell the smell of alcohol on his breath.

"I'm not a child. Who the hell are you to teach me anything? I have a master's degree and you're an unqualified clown. I'm sick of hearing you tell me how you're the best in the world at everything, or telling me how intelligent you are."

"Nobody knows more about the Nazis than me," Simeon remonstrated.

Chapter Six

"Yes, they do – and even they didn't, who is that going to impress? It just makes you sound like a right-wing dickhead."

"No, it doesn't," Simeon said. "We have to learn from history."

"And what have you learned? That everyone in the world speaks English if you only shout the words loudly enough at them? You seem to always take an opposing view from the consensus and I've realised that you do it in the hope that people will say 'Wow, that Simeon Danton is so smart!'"

"I think you'll find all the educated people agree with me," Simeon said, pulling up his jogging bottoms and tightening its drawstring.

"Yes - all those lucky ladies you've romanced with your anecdotes about the Nazis."

"Look, you're nothing special," he said. "Other than me, who's going to want you?"

"And that's the way to make someone feel special, is it?"

"Oh, shut it," Simeon said, gesturing to Cassandra to close her mouth by snapping his fingers against his thumb.

"What's more, I've been to see Anna."

Chapter Six

"You what!"

"I don't need your permission to go and see her, either."

"You wouldn't like it if I was going to see some old tart I'd slept with, would you?" Simeon asked.

"No one understands a woman's needs like another woman," Cassandra said. "Why does everything have to be about sex with you? Now I know a bit more about you, I'm surprised you didn't turn up on our first date with your jeans round your ankles to save time!"

"You bitch," again Simeon lunged at Cassandra, lifting his leg as though he were about to kick her. Cassandra pushed him away but the combination of alcohol and being caught off-balance, caused him to topple backwards down the stairs.

Quickly, Cassandra grabbed a few clothes and tossed them into a holdall, all the while trying to block out the fearful groaning assailing her from the bottom of the stairs.

"We need to ring an ambulance," said one of Simeon's friends.

Chapter Six

Only then did Cassandra realise that the fall Simeon had taken down the stairs had been serious and that it had resulted in him lying motionless, a wound on his head staining the carpet beneath him.

"Oh, shit," Cassandra said as she descended the stairs, her voice shaking with fear.

"What happened?" said a second of Simeon's friends.

"He lost his balance on the stairs," Cassandra said.

"Did I bollocks! You pushed me," Simeon said. By now, he had rolled onto his back and was trying to sit upright.

"I'm going - I won't be back," Cassandra said, relieved that Simeon wasn't gravely injured but pleased that he was in no state to prevent her from leaving.

Quickly, she moved to her car, throwing her belongings into the passenger seat, and slamming the driver's-side door shut.

She turned the key to start the engine and heard nothing but a click.

"Don't do this now, you bastard," she said, banging the steering wheel with the palms of her

Chapter Six

hand. She turned the key again just as the house door opened and Simeon stood in its portal, a towel wrapped around his head. Cassandra turned the key a third time and the car's engine started. Cassandra slammed the car into reverse, then through the gears, grinding the clutch in her haste. Within seconds Cassandra had left the street, breathing a sigh of relief. Not long after that, she was on the road back to the Wye Valley, the nineteenth century, and Lucius.

Chapter Seven

After the attention Cassandra's car had caused on her previous visit, she decided to park it outside the nineteenth century and walk the rest of the way on foot. Again, the village seemed quiet. How different it must have been in eighteen thirty-one when a doctor at the larger village nearby wrote to a minister in Bristol stating his concern about the spiritual state of the villagers and the predilection for drinking, gambling, and fighting.

At first, Cassandra's presence caused no attention as there was no one from the nineteenth century to see her.

A different ferryman to the one that had ferried her across the river the previous day was working today and although he looked askance at her, Cassandra didn't feel too alarmed at his interest.

As she walked along the banks of the river, she spotted a figure in the distance, walking toward her. When they got within such a distance that their mutual features rendered them recognisable to one another she could see the alarm on the woman's face. It couldn't be the

Chapter Seven

clothes she was wearing, Cassandra thought, as there was such a look of terror on her face one might be forgiven for thinking she had, as Lucius had suggested about the reaction Cassandra's appearance had elicited in the other villagers, seen a ghost. As if that wasn't enough, the woman began screaming and crying before running from the field in a state of terror.

Cassandra finally came to the entrance to the ascending path that led through the ancient wood and began to make her way to the old shop that lay deep within.

"I'm back," she said, pushing open the shop door.

"I've missed you," Lucius said, rising from his seat and coming to greet her. Taking her hands in his, he kissed them; then, taking a step forward, he kissed her lips.

"I know this will sound strange," Cassandra began, "but even though we only met a few days ago, I can't now imagine how life would be without you – or even remember how lonely I was until I met you," she confided, tears filling her eyes.

Chapter Seven

"I know, I feel the same way about you - you feel as if you're a part of me," Lucius said, kissing her again.

"I don't ever want to return to the twenty-first century," Cassandra said. "It was horrible. I don't have any place to call home," she added, before pausing. "May I stay here – with you?"

"I'd be heartbroken if you didn't," Lucius replied. "Let me get your bag," he added, picking up Cassandra's bag and walking to the room in which he had read Cassandra's fortune.

"Where can I stay?" Cassandra asked.

There was a pause for a moment before Lucius turned and spoke.

"I was hoping you would stay with me," he replied.

"Yes, I was also hoping for that," Cassandra said, smiling a broad smile as Lucius led them to the bottom of a short and narrow staircase.

"This way," he nodded, gesturing to the stairs that led to his bedroom with his free arm, as he bade Cassandra walk in front of him.

A few seconds later the pair were on the cottage landing.

Chapter Seven

"This is it," Lucius said, allowing Cassandra to enter first.

"What a beautiful room!" she exclaimed, walking to the room's open window, and wallowing in the sunlight and sound of birdsong as she looked down the sylvan valley.

Lucius let go of the bag and walked toward Cassandra, wrapping an arm around her waist, and standing alongside her. As she had not heard his silent approach, his touch surprised her. Turning to face him, in the sunshine his eyes sparkled. Lucius also turned and raised his hand to her face, tenderly touching her cheek before drawing her toward him and kissing her again.

As much as Cassandra wanted to satisfy her frustrated desires, she held those desires in check knowing that the anticipation of such delights would make those delights all the more exquisite when the wellspring of her passion could no longer be held in check.

"I had such a strange experience as I was coming here," she said. "A woman in the field seemed terrified of me."

"Like she'd seen a ghost?" Lucius asked.

Chapter Seven

"Yes! How did you know I was going to say that?"

"You're not of their time," he explained. Have you ever seen a ghost?" he asked.

"Yes, I have," Cassandra replied, feeling a little coy at the admission.

"Those are people from what we think of as the past that have strayed into what we think of as the present. You, on the other hand, are a visitor from what we think of as the present into what we think of as the past," he explained. "Not only that," he began, before walking to a dressing table. "There's this," he said, removing a sepia photograph and giving it to Cassandra.

"It's me!" she exclaimed.

"Remember that I said we were lovers at the time of the French Revolution? And again in the nineteenth century? Well, this is the nineteenth century and we were lovers until last year when your husband found out about our clandestine affair and killed you. That's you in that photograph," Lucius said, pointing at the photograph in Cassandra's hand.

Chapter Seven

"Whoa, I was murdered? What happened in the eighteenth century?" she asked, forgetting that Lucius had already told her.

"We were lovers," he began. "And what a lover! I had never known such passion. It still breaks my heart to remember but we were caught up in the French Revolution and you were killed."

"I was killed twice?" Cassandra said, slumping into a chair and looking at Lucius with bewilderment. "How come you weren't able to predict those murders and save me?"

"I didn't dare to look at what future you and I had together, lest I found out that we would be parted. I waited over a century for you to return to me, and return you did," he said, pausing for breath. "Sometimes, knowing what fates await us isn't a good thing."

"I suppose," Cassandra said.

"This is a lawless area that had – and still has - criminals and the unwanted from both Wales and the Forest of Dean coming here to make a living on the dock. You arrived here last year from Wales, the wife or such a criminal. We met in the village and our souls recognised one another," he said, pausing again to regroup his thoughts. "You

Chapter Seven

know how you can meet someone and instantly dislike them?"

"You disliked me!"

"No, no – quite the opposite," Lucius replied.

"That's alright then – please, go on," said Cassandra, still unsure of where the conversation was leading.

"Well, you know how you can meet someone and instantly dislike them - and then meet someone else and instantly feel that you like them?"

"Yes,' said Cassandra, moving from her seat and sitting on the edge of the bed.

"Well, if you're lucky, once in a lifetime you'll meet someone and know that somewhere, somehow, you were destined to be together – forever."

"But the photo?" Cassandra asked, looking down at the photo in her lap.

"Yes, you were killed and I spent a century desolate and inconsolable at losing you. You saw my home when first you visited and how it looked? I had given up on life – then you came back to me and gave me a reason to live again.

Chapter Seven

Somehow, you slipped back in time so even though I waited over a century for you, you have returned to a time little more than a year after your death – or, I should say, the death of the woman in the photo – and a century before you, the beautiful woman sat on the edge of my bed, was born."

"That's very kind of you but you seem very taken with her," Cassandra said, feeling a pang of jealousy.

"Not her, you - it was always you. I'm more than taken with you," he paused, before kneeling in front of Cassandra and taking her hands in his. "I love you," he said, looking at Cassandra to gauge her reaction.

"It makes crazy sense in some ways as I can look at you and feel like I've known you forever. You feel like the missing part of me that makes me feel complete," Cassandra said, whispering the words and looking at Lucius for his reaction.

Lucius stood and moved toward Cassandra and, once again, held her hands in his, lifting them so that Cassandra rose to her feet. Gently, he touched her neck, brushing aside her hair.

Chapter Seven

Leaning forward, he kissed her neck before looking up at her face and kissing her lips.

"You don't know how good that feels," Cassandra said. "I want you."

Slowly, Lucius unbuttoned her top, sliding a hand underneath it and then running his hand down the length of the soft skin of her back.

"Oh God, that feels so nice," she whispered.

"As nice as this?" Lucius asked, kissing her neck where it joined her chest, slowly working his way down until he came to her exposed breast.

"Don't stop, please don't stop," Cassandra gasped, clutching Lucius by the hair in order to draw him even closer to her. His warm breath on her nipple caused it to harden beneath his lips, as Lucius flicked his tongue over it and gently sucked.

"Oh God, I want you inside me," Cassandra whispered.

Lucius unbuttoned Cassandra's jeans and slid them down, and helped her step out of them. Then, standing, he ran his hand down the sides of her bare torso. Cassandra tore at his shirt, baring his chest and pressing herself against him.

Chapter Seven

Lucius again ran his hand down Cassandra's back until he reached her hips, pausing a second before slowly easing down her underwear. Pressing himself against her, Cassandra touched him through the thin fabric of his trousers. Easing the buttons open, she gasped as she felt him stiffen at her delicate touch.

Cassandra sank to her knees and took his erection into her mouth, before flicking her tongue over it and running her lips along the shaft until it glistened.

"I want to taste you, too," he said, lifting her to her feet and laying her down on the bed. Slowly, he eased her thighs apart and gave her clitoris a gentle caress before bringing the fingers he'd used to his mouth and licking them; then he tenderly trailed those same fingers down her body, letting one wet finger slip inside her.

Starting with her face, he moved his lips down her quivering body, savouring the taste on her skin as it glistened in the heat of the room.

Tenderly, he parted her lips and, once again, brought the fingers he'd used on her to his mouth and licked them. By now, Cassandra could feel the stubble on his face on her stomach and moving

Chapter Seven

down. Lucius savoured the taste and again slipped a finger inside his lover as he began licking her, running his tongue across her clitoris until she quivered beneath each lingual caress.

"Straddle me," he whispered, a few minutes later as he lay down, his back on the bed. "Maybe you can suck me as I lick you."

"Ooh, a sixty-nine," Cassandra said.

"*Oui, un soixante-neuf,*" Lucius replied.

"Oh God, how could I refuse," Cassandra replied.

Now that he was lying flat on the bed, Cassandra straddled his face, then bent forward. Taking his erection in her mouth, she began to suck.

In turn, Lucius grabbed a hold of her bare buttocks and buried his face between her pouting lips.

Gasping with delight, Cassandra returned to her duties and again took Lucius in her mouth, sliding her mouth up and down his rigid erection.

After months of frustration, the intimate pleasure of bare skin on bare skin was too much for them.

Chapter Seven

"Oh God, I'm cumming," Cassandra gushed, just a few minutes later, taking her mouth away from Lucius' erection and masturbating him as her whole body shuddered with an orgasm.

"I'm about to cum as well," Lucius said. "Don't worry, I won't cum in your mouth," he gasped.

"You can if you want - I came in yours!" she giggled.

"Only if you kiss me with it still on your lips," Lucius teased.

"Yes, with pleasure," Cassandra said excitedly, frantically pulling at him until he ejaculated, a little landing on her cheek and lips and the rest into her warm mouth.

Lucius groaned, his back arched, and he closed his eyes.

"Kiss me," he said.

Swiftly, Cassandra turned and kissed Lucius deeply, passionately.

"I could taste myself on your lips," she giggled.

"And I could taste myself on yours," he laughed. "It's been too long," he added. "My God, I've missed you."

Chapter Eight

The next few hours were spent in one another's arms, lost in a post-orgasmic torpor.

"I need you again," Cassandra murmured, taking hold of Lucius' member and giggling as it stiffened in her hand, each caress causing Lucius to groan with pleasure. "I can hear your heartbeat," she said, resting her head on his bare chest.

"I want you to fuck me," Lucius said, his voice almost inaudible. "Get on top."

"Ooh, my favourite position," Cassandra said, as she straddled Lucius. Parting her lips, she rubbed Lucius' erection between them until it glistened; then, slowly lowered herself onto it until it was completely inside her.

"Oh God, that feels so good," she gasped, grinding her pelvis against him.

Lucius opened his eyes and reached up to caress Cassandra's breasts, pinching her nipples.

"Pinch them harder!" she panted.

"*Oui, mademoiselle,*" he replied.

"Harder – it makes me want to cum,"

"This hard?" Lucius said, squeezing a little harder, and harder still.

Chapter Eight

"Oh God, that feels amazing," Cassandra gasped, grinding her pelvis into the pelvis of her lover.

"It feels wonderful," he gasped.

The two lovers' ground against one another until the heat of the room made them glisten.

"Don't you cum mind," she said. "Not until I've had my orgasm."

"Anything for you, dear lady," Lucius replied.

"Oh God, you make me feel so full - I'm cumming," Cassandra moaned, leaning forward to French kiss Lucius, her breath hot on his lips, her breasts pressed against his chest.

"Turn over," Lucius said. "Now, I'm going to fuck you - hard!"

"On all fours?" Cassandra asked, her eyes brightening at the thought.

"Yes," Lucius said, lifting Cassandra off his swollen, rigid member and moving behind her. Moving his erection between her wet lips, he pushed himself deep inside.

"Oh God, you're so deep. You're hitting my G-spot - I can feel your balls banging against me," she gasped, taking her hand, and cupping her

Chapter Eight

lover's genitals, urging him to thrust even more deeply than before.

Lucius leaned over Cassandra and reached around to massage her breasts, all the while thrusting himself in and out of her. Steadying himself, he removed a hand and ran it up and down the soft skin of Cassandra's back.

"Cum inside me," she begged. "I want to feel you cum deep inside me and then oozing out," she gasped.

Taking both hands and parting her buttocks, Lucius thrust again, thrusting as deep as he could and causing Cassandra to let out a squeal of delight.

"I'm going to cum," Lucius said, looking down at his erection as it slid in and out of his lover.

"Yes, give it to me," Cassandra gasped.

Lucius grunted and leaned over Cassandra, turning her head so he could French kiss her as he ejaculated deep inside her.

"I'm cumming," he gasped into her open mouth.

Chapter Eight

"I can feel it! I can feel it pulsing," Cassandra gasped, reaching between her lips, and touching herself.

Slowly, Lucius withdrew and Cassandra slumped to her side in ecstatic exhaustion.

"I'm a very oral person," she said, slipping a finger inside herself before bringing it to her mouth and licking it with eager delight.

"And me," Lucius said, leaning forward and kissing his lover, tasting the taste of their union with the same pleasure as before.

"That was amazing," Cassandra whispered. "I want to do *everything* with you."

"And I want to do everything with you – use my body like you would your own. No need to ask if it's alright, just do it," he replied, breathing so heavily that he had to rest his head on the pillow of his bed.

"The same goes for me – do anything you want. I want to do everything with you," Cassandra replied, leaning forward to kiss him.

The morning sun of the new day now penetrated the window and fell upon the two naked forms that lay entwined, before Cassandra moved.

Chapter Eight

"I suppose we'd better get up," she said. "What shall we do today? I'm in a new century and would love to see what it's like."

"Of course. Shall we go for a picnic? I can show you the area," Lucius suggested.

"That sounds nice," Cassandra replied, climbing from the bed, and walking to a dressing table where stood a jug of water and a large china basin. "Just let me have a quick wash and I can make us some food," she added.

Lucius got dressed and as he buttoned his shirt he walked toward Cassandra; moving aside her hair, he kissed her cheek.

"I've missed you so much," he said, his eyes glistening as tears of happiness began to fill them.

"You're the one I've waited a lifetime to meet," Cassandra said, wrapping her arm around him before pulling him toward her and kissing his lips.

"What should I wear?" she asked, remembering the attention her modern-day clothes had caused the day before.

"I have a wardrobe full of clothes that I bought for you before you were taken from me

Chapter Eight

last year," Lucius said. "They've never been worn," he added."

"Ooh, let me see!" Cassandra said with excitement.

"The dresses are simple as I didn't like the bustle that was popular a few years ago," Lucius said, opening a wardrobe door. "I think you'll like the undergarments! They're muslin and decorated with bands of lace. Suspenders replaced garters a few years ago and can be buttoned to your corset. Drawers – or should I say knickerbockers – are in that drawer there," he said, pointing at a drawer on the dressing table. "The shirt is like mine - with a high collar - but it's definitely a woman's shirt, I promise! There's also a double-breasted waistcoat or two. I think you may need a jacket in case the weather changes so there's one or two of those, too. They have those 'leg of mutton' sleeves that seem very popular at the moment," he said, pausing. "There are also some nice black stockings in those drawers over there," he said, pointing to a chest of drawers. "Oh, and boots over there," he added, pointing to a few pairs of high buttoned boots that sat alongside laced-up shoes that had large buckles decorating the front of them.

Chapter Eight

Lucius smiled at Cassandra, moved to the door and descended the stairs.

Within an hour, Cassandra had both dressed and finished packing a small hamper, before moving from the kitchen to the shop, where Lucius sat behind a counter.

"Ready when you are," Cassandra said, as Lucius rose to his feet.

"You look lovely!" he said, moving toward Cassandra. Looking her up and down, he leaned in to kiss her on the cheek.

"I found a few dresses that look like they might have been worn by a Can-can girl at the *Folies Bergère* so I decided to wear one of those," Cassandra said.

"And you look very beautiful in it, I must say," Lucius said. "Here, let me carry that," he added, taking the hamper from Cassandra.

The two then walked hand in hand to the door, their footsteps sounding on the shop's old floorboards.

"I'd better lock the door," Lucius said, as he opened the door for Cassandra to exit.

Chapter Eight

"What a lovely day," Cassandra said, squinting into the sunshine that oozed over the valley like warm honey.

The two made their way down the steep steps and narrow path, over ancient stones, and knotted roots thick with damp moss and lichen.

"Here we are," Lucius said, taking Cassandra's fragile hand in his as the two began their walk alongside the beautiful river.

"Where are you going to take me?" Cassandra asked.

"Let's just stroll a while, shall we? On a day like this who needs a plan?"

Within an hour, the two had reached the village; Cassandra gazed up.

"No wires," she said. "I really *am* in the nineteenth century."

Chapter Nine

As the two entered the village, Cassandra's attention was first drawn to the road. Gone was the tarmac of the twenty-first century; here was a road little changed since the Middle Ages.

"There's the weird guy that was looking at me on the ferry," said Cassandra, leaning towards Lucius in order to whisper the words into his ear.

"Which one?" he asked, turning his back on the three labourers that were looking at them, their soiled, tattered clothing and dirty faces giving them an unsettling appearance.

"The one in the middle," Cassandra replied.

"That's John Wintour - he's a cousin of the husband you had that murdered you last year."

"No wonder he's looking at me – he must think he's seen a ghost," said Cassandra, feeling uneasy as the thought about how he might react.

"And what happened to my husband?" asked Cassandra.

"He was hung," Lucius said. "He had quite a criminal record," he added, after seeing the look of shock on Cassandra's face.

Chapter Nine

"Oh great!" Cassandra said disconsolately. "I always seemed to pick such idiots before I meet you."

"Thank you, sweetheart. Don't worry, he's not that bright. He seems to recognise you but it doesn't look like he can remember where from," Lucius said, holding Cassandra's hand a little tighter as they passed the dock workers who, by now, had sat down near the banks of the river. All three fell silent as the lovers approached.

"See, he didn't say a thing," said Lucius.

Passing the old pub and taking a right turn as they came to the medieval Monks' Hall, the two continued to hands and as they walked up a small lane and into a darkened wood.

"Ooh, I like it here," Cassandra said, sunlight filtering through the leaves and falling on her pretty face, still a little flushed from the sexual rigours she had enjoyed earlier that morning.

"There's an interesting viewpoint up here," Lucius said. "It's named The Devil's Pulpit."

"Oh, I've heard of that! Isn't that where the Devil is supposed to have appeared and preached his gospel to the monks tending the abbey gardens in the Middle Ages?" asked Cassandra.

Chapter Nine

"Yes, that's the one. This is a land of myth and magic - and why I chose to live here," he said, as they climbed the steep path through the sylvan glade.

"I think it must have also been the place where Wordsworth sat when he wrote his poem about the abbey," Cassandra said.

"William Wordsworth? Yes, I remember him coming here. In fact, he visited the place twice – once in seventeen ninety-three and then again five years later. The first time he had written a poem about a child that lived in a cottage in a churchyard at Goodrich – about seventeen miles from here," Lucius said.

"You met Wordsworth! That's incredible," said Cassandra.

"I also met Percy and Mary Shelley when they visited the area in eighteen fifteen. They'd come to look at a house but it was too small for their needs and wasn't even half-built and so they moved on to Europe to see Byron."

"Ah, and there they had their *haunted summer*," Cassandra replied.

"Their what?" Lucius asked.

Chapter Nine

"Their haunted summer. They spent it at the Villa Diodati on the shores of Lake Geneva but it did nothing but rain and so Byron suggested that they all write a ghost story. Byron's physician – Doctor Polidori – wrote *The Vampyre* and Mary Shelley wrote *Frankenstein*," Cassandra said, remembering her studies on the subject at university.

"I liked Percy Shelley. Did you know that he was also a vegetarian? I also liked his liberal politics," Lucius said.

"This is so weird," Cassandra said. "Who's ever going to believe me if I tell them that I know a man that knew Shelley!"

"Such a tragic death, too," Lucius said.

"Didn't he drown?"

"Yes, and being an atheist, they buried his body on the beach. A few days later they had second thoughts and went to find the body but none of them could remember where on the beach he was buried. So, they all began digging and one of them hit the front of his head with a mattock, removing a portion of his skull," Lucius said, gesturing with his hand how the mattock must have opened wide the front of the poet's head.

Chapter Nine

"Oh my God, is that true?" Cassandra said.

"Absolutely," Lucius replied. "His heart was also cut from his chest to give to Mary, who kept it with her for the rest of her life."

"How macabre," Cassandra replied, as Lucius stopped to catch his breath, before continuing the steep climb uphill.

"They had built a funeral pyre to cremate his body but as the flames grew higher," he continued, "the heat caused the flap of bone at the front of his head to pop open, whereupon his brains were seen to bubble, like 'stew in a cauldron.'"

Cassandra, sensitive to the idea of skulls being opened and brains exposed, given her personal experience in such matters, made no mention of what Lucius had said.

"Mary Shelley's mother is something of a hero of mine," said Cassandra.

"Mary Wollstonecraft?" queried Lucius.

"Yes - a great advocate for women's rights."

"Here we are," Lucius said, stopping at a promontory of rock that jutted out over the trees below it, thus allowing visitors a view of the abbey far below.

Chapter Nine

"So, we're in England and that's Wales?" asked Cassandra.

"Yes, that's right."

"I love it here! It can't have changed much in centuries," Cassandra said, turning with arms outstretched.

"No, it hasn't - the docks have all but gone, as have the pubs, the whores, and the 'rustic pursuits' that they once enjoyed."

"Rustic pursuits?" queried Cassandra.

"Fighting, gambling, dancing, whoring," he paused. "And cockfighting,"

"Bastards," Cassandra said, her smile turning to a scowl.

"I agree - at one time I hoped to change them but it was like casting pearls before swine."

"I'm a vegan," said Cassandra.

"I know – so am I. We've known each other for centuries, remember?"

"Why is it that you don't eat meat?" Cassandra asked.

"I don't feast on corpses," Lucius replied, causing Cassandra to throw her arms around him and kiss him.

"That's exactly how I feel," Cassandra said.

Chapter Nine

"I've missed you so much," Lucius said, looking at Cassandra and wondering how he survived a century without her. Taking Cassandra by the hand, he led her back down the path from whence they had come.

"Let's find somewhere where we can rest awhile, enjoy the view, and have a bite to eat," said Lucius.

"I can't wait to feel the sun on my face – I've spent too long in lockdown," Cassandra said, squeezing Lucius' hand. "A field would be nice."

Silently, the two walked, each knowing that the feelings they had for one another could stay unspoken, knowing that such feelings aren't easily expressed with words.

Pausing for a moment, Lucius pointed at a yew tree.

"See that tree?" he asked.

"Yes, what about it?"

"That was growing here when I first came to this place in the eleventh century," he said, smiling at the tree as though he had seen the face of an old friend.

"That's amazing," Cassandra said. "I've read about yews and why there are so many in

Chapter Nine

churchyards but can't quite remember as it was a long time ago," she added.

"Would you like me to tell you?" Lucius said.

"Yes, please."

"The yew has been associated with death - and the journey of the soul from this life to the next - for thousands of years. As such, it was sacred to Hecate, the Ancient Greek Goddess of Death, Witchcraft and Necromancy. It was also thought that yews purified the dead as they entered the underworld of Hades. The druids in Celtic Wales also saw yews as sacred, planting them close to their temples as they used yews in their death rituals. Because it is such a long-lived tree, it came to represent eternal life.

"Many churches were built on the sites of what were once Celtic temples. As we might expect, Christianity borrowed a lot of pagan imagery and beliefs when trying to convert those pagans. In fact, in the year six-hundred and one Pope Gregory suggested that places of pagan worship could simply be converted into Christian churches."

Chapter Nine

"I love things like this," Cassandra said. "Visiting old churches and seeing yews in the cemetery puts us so close to ancient history."

"Very near, given every moment in time – past, present, and future – is happening right now," Lucius replied.

"And I'm proof that the people we once loved are never more than a fingertip away," Cassandra said, touching Lucius' hand.

Lucius stopped and smiled.

"There was another reason why Christians viewed yews as holy, and that was because the heart of the tree is red, while its sap is white - and as every Catholic knows, these colours symbolise the blood and body of Christ. It's also a very hardy tree that can thrive on apparently infertile soil so it also suggested rebirth and resurrection," he added, stopping, and looking about him.

"What is it?" Cassandra asked.

"This is Offa's Dyke," Lucius said.

"Now I've also heard of this but can't remember the details. What is it?"

"A large earthwork border that's named after Offa, the Anglo-Saxon king of Mercia from seven sixty-seven until seven ninety-six who,

Chapter Nine

legend has it, ordered its construction. It was the old border between Anglian Mercia and the Welsh kingdom of Powys."

"Wow, that's so old," said Cassandra.

"Older than that," Lucius said, "as it was started in the fifth century. It had a ditch on the Welsh side with the soil from that piled into a bank on the Mercian side. Throughout its entire length, the Dyke provides an uninterrupted view from Mercia into Wales. It is to Wales, what Hadrian's Wall is to the Scottish," he said, pausing for a moment. "Thirty years ago, the writer George Borrow wrote that it was customary for the English to cut off the ears of every Welshman who was found to the east of the dyke, and for the Welsh to hang every Englishman that they found to the west of it."

"Crazy!" said Cassandra. "And what about the French?" she added, giving Lucius a wink.

"Ah, that he didn't say," Lucius said, kissing Cassandra's cheek. "This would be a nice spot," he added, setting himself down at the top of a steep pasture that afforded them panoramic views of the village and the valley.

Chapter Nine

"I've found a place I can call home," sitting down and gazing into the distance.

"Are you sure?" Lucius asked.

"Why do you ask?" Cassandra said, a little hurt to think that he did not feel the same way about her as she did about him.

"Because you've strayed from your moment in time into this one. Many people go missing every year and some are never heard from again. It's not always the case that they've gone some *place* else, but some *time* else. These gateways to the past – or the future – don't stay open for long. I would be heartbroken to lose you again but you had your life in the twenty-first century. What if the doorway in time closes and leaves you stuck here?"

"I don't care! I hated my life in the twenty-first century. I was an only child and both my parents are now dead. All I had was an oaf that was using me whereas here, here I have you," she said, then paused for a moment. "And this," she gestured with a sweeping wave of her hand at the lush green of the verdurous valley that lay before them.

Chapter Nine

"I couldn't be happier - each day apart from you is a day to be endured," Lucius replied, taking Cassandra's hand and kissing the back of her fingers.

The lovers paused a while and ate their picnic. Unbeknown to Lucius, Cassandra had also packed a bottle of wine.

"Look what we have here!" she said, holding it aloft and smiling.

"Well, we'd certainly better drink that," Lucius said, opening it and pouring them each a drink.

After the bottle had been quaffed, Cassandra sidled up to Lucius and rested her head on his shoulder. He, in turn, held a buttercup under her chin.

"Let's go back to the river. It's such a nice day, we can have a paddle," she said, playfully running her fingers through Lucius' hair. Standing, he reached out a hand and helped Cassandra to her feet, before both descended the hill, luxuriating on the panorama that lay before them.

Chapter Nine

"It's so beautiful here. It reminds me of that Johnny Depp film *Chocolat* – have you seen it?" said Cassandra asked.

"Johnny who?" Lucius replied.

"Sorry, I forgot that he won't even be born for another seventy-three years! He's an actor."

"An actor? Like Sir Henry Irving?" Lucius asked.

"Something like that, yes," Cassandra replied. "To think, I wasn't even going to visit your shop. If I hadn't been bored of staring at the same four walls – and going mad because of the pandemic sweeping the country – I might never have met you."

"Met me *again*," Lucius said.

"Yes, sorry – again."

"Life can change in an instant," Lucius replied.

The village was strangely silent as they passed through it with only a few children playing games in the street.

"It's nice to see them out rather than sat at home on their Xbox," Cassandra said.

"Xbox?" Lucius asked.

Chapter Nine

"It doesn't matter," Cassandra said. "It's just something else from my time that's creating a generation that doesn't know how to talk to one another – Lucius," she added. "I feel a little tipsy."

Soon the lovers were both by the slow-flowing river. Occasional bushes and the odd tree stood along its banks. Spying a gap between one clump of bushes and another, Cassandra pulled Lucius between them.

"Guess what?" she said, kissing him.

"What?"

"I'm almost naked under this dress," she said, unbuttoning it and letting it fall to the ground. "See, I told you I was a little bit tipsy!"

"I love seeing you naked," Lucius said.

"Thank you" Do you think I have a nice bum?" Cassandra said, as she slid down her underwear and, turning, slapped one of her bare cheeks.

"Callipygian perfection, my dear," Lucius said, falling to his knees and kissing the cheek that Cassandra had just slapped. Sidling up to Lucius who, by now, had returned to his feet, Cassandra began unbuttoning his shirt with one hand and rubbing his groin with the other.

Chapter Nine

"That wine has made me a little frisky," she giggled.

"Me too," Lucius replied.

Soon, the two stood naked, holding each other close as flickering shadows of light and dark dappled upon them as the sun bounced off ripples in the water.

Cassandra led Lucius down to the water's edge and stepped in as Lucius followed her.

"I already feel like I've been here a lifetime," she said, kissing Lucius and gently massaging his manhood beneath the water. Again, she giggled as it stiffened at her tender touch.

"I want you inside me," she whispered coquettishly, straddling him and sliding down his rigid staff.

"Feels so good," Lucius gasped as the cool water splashed around them. Taking Cassandra's nipples between his fingers he gave them a squeeze, causing Cassandra to quiver in paroxysms of delight.

"Don't cum! I want to tease you - I want your balls to ache for me so much that you can hardly walk back to the shop! And then as soon as we get there, I want you to just bend me over and fuck

Chapter Nine

me hard as you have to have me there and then for being such a tease and making your balls ache," she softly laughed.

"But I want to cum now," Lucius implored, sucking Cassandra's nipple, and looking up at her with his bright blue eyes.

"Too bad," Cassandra said, dismounting and masturbating Lucius beneath the waters of the cool rivers. "I love your big balls," she added, giving them a rub. "Want to go back to the shop and give me a good seeing to?"

Chapter Ten

Back at the shop, Lucius closed the door and strode toward Cassandra, kissing her passionately as she massaged his groin through the fabric of his trousers before unbuttoning them. It wasn't long before her nimble fingers began masturbating him. Now that he was fully erect, she turned around, lifted her dress, and bent over to expose her bare backside.

"Come on, Lucius, slide it into me," she said, looking around at him, widening her eyes and blowing him a kiss. "I've dropped my knickers for you – now this ass is all yours!"

Lucius took a hold of his penis and stroked his hand back and forth, lusting at the sight that awaited him.

"I love watching you masturbate – it really turns me on," Cassandra said, spreading her buttocks so Lucius could more easily slide himself inside her. She gasped as it entered her, his thrusts soon becoming so hard and deep that she had to steady herself by bending over the shop counter.

"Come on, Lucius," she said. "Give it to me! Teach me a lesson for making your balls ache" she added, reaching between her legs to pleasure

Chapter Ten

herself. "I'm a bad girl and bad girls need to be taught a lesson!"

"Yes they do," Lucius said, playfully smacking her bare backside, then clenching his teeth in ecstasy, digging his fingers into Cassandra's backside and leaving red marks as he kneaded the flesh beneath them.

"See, I told you that you'd want me even more if I made you wait. Come on, fuck me, you dirty bastard! Use me! Call me a whore," she gasped.

"You like that, you whore?" he said, thrusting hard, before bending over Cassandra to mound Cassandra's exposed breasts and pinch her nipples so hard that she moaned in pleasure.

"I want you to cum inside me," she said. "Cum hard and deep - fill me up with your hot cum," she moaned.

Gasping, he brushed aside Cassandra's hair and kissed her neck.

"Bite me," she panted, as Lucius continued to thrust his engorged member in and out of his lover, biting the flesh of her tender neck where it joined her shoulder. "Oh God," she gasped.

Chapter Ten

"Harder," she gasped, rubbing between her legs a little faster.

Lucius continued to pound and as he felt a wave of orgasmic pleasure shudder through Cassandra, he bit down even harder.

"Yes! Yes! Oh God, I've missed you," she gasped.

"You're incredible, Cass," Lucius said, watching as Cassandra turned, sank to her knees, and took his member into her mouth.

"I told you, I'm a very oral person," she said, licking Lucius' semi-erect penis.

"Sorry to bother you – are you open?" came a voice behind them.

Unbeknown to the lovers, in their frenzied passion, a local had been watching them the whole time.

"Give me a moment," Lucius said, tucking his manhood back into his trousers as Cassandra wiped her lips with her finger before covering her chest, and standing up so that her dress fell back down to her calves.

"Now, how may I help you?" Lucius said, turning to see that the local had left them.

Chapter Ten

"I hope he enjoyed the show," Cassandra said, laughing and taking a step toward Lucius to kiss him.

"How could he not with someone as beautiful you as the star performer," Lucius replied, wrapping his arm around Cassandra's waist, and drawing her near to him. "I know that I keep saying it but, God, I've missed you," he said, kissing her face.

Chapter Eleven

The next day, the two lovers once again awoke to the sound of birdsong outside the little cottage window. Cassandra gently pulled by the blankets and stepped from the bed to peek through the panes at the world outside, sighing with pleasure at the view of the woodland before her.

"What's the matter?" Lucius said, stirring from his slumber and sleepily looking about the room after his outstretched arm had sought Cassandra and found nothing more than the pillow on which she had lain.

"Nothing's the matter – nothing could be more perfect," she replied.

"Good!" Lucius replied, yawning, and stretching his arms as he sat on the edge of the bed. "What would you like to do today?" he asked.

"Aside from making love to you?" Cassandra teased, walking across the room to give Lucius a kiss.

"I was hoping you'd say that," he said, reaching around her and squeezing her bare backside before pulling her close and kissing her stomach.

Chapter Eleven

"I may need to go back to the twenty-first century as I've forgotten my pill," she replied, stroking his face with her hand, and running her thumb across his lips.

"Pill? Are you ill?" Lucius asked, concerned that Cassandra was unwell.

"No, my contraceptive pill," she said smiling and running her fingers through his hair.

"They have a pill for it? My, how times have changed," he said.

"Well, we don't want to be using condoms, do we? I want to feel skin on skin!" Cassandra said coquettishly, leaning forward to kiss Lucius' handsome face.

"Prophylactics? They sell some vulcanised rubber ones in the village."

"Really? Since when? I thought that contraception was a real problem for nineteenth-century women," Cassandra said, a little dumbfounded.

"For about twenty years, I think," Lucius replied, looking around for his clothes. "I've not used them but a customer of mine likened them to trying to scratch your foot while you're still wearing a shoe," he laughed.

Chapter Eleven

"Well, we certainly won't be using them then," said Cassandra, wrinkling her nose in mock disgust.

Lucius paced around the room, looking for his clothes, clothes he had thrown off in the heat of passion after the previous day's sex in the shop had progressed upstairs.

"Have you seen my boots?" he asked.

"Over there," Cassandra said, pulling on a shirt. "Have you seen my underwear?" she asked.

"Up there," Lucius said, pointing at the stained-glass lampshade that hung by a chain from the ceiling and Cassandra's underwear hanging from it.

"Sorry," said Cassandra, laughing at the memory as she climbed on the bed to retrieve them. "I still think it would be best if I head back to the twenty-first century and pick up a few things, my pill included," she added, stepping into her underwear before climbing down from the brass bed.

"Will you be safe?" Lucius asked, concerned that Cassandra's former partner may cause trouble.

Chapter Eleven

"Why do you ask? Are you worried that I may not be able to find a way back here – and you?" she asked, her forehead creasing into a frown. "Maybe you can come with me," she added.

"Maybe," Lucius said, as they dressed. After dressing, the two made their way downstairs.

"Will it be okay to lock up the shop for a few hours?" she asked.

"Yes, it will be fine. It's not as if I'm going to lose any customers, given I have so few of them."

"I remember," Cassandra said, interrupting Lucius and curtailing what he was going to say.

"I don't understand," he responded.

"When I first came here you said you hadn't had a customer in years."

"'Years'? That was back in the future," Lucius replied. "Is that what happens to me?" he asked, looking sad.

"Don't you ever divine your own future?" Cassandra asked.

"No, definitely not. Imagine if I had done such a thing in the eighteenth century and found out I would have to wait another century for you to return to me. By not doing it, I can wake up

Chapter Eleven

every day and think 'Ah, perhaps this will be the day she'll return to me," he said. "Life has been very lonely," he added.

"Yes, but then I came back into your life," Cassandra said, brushing his cheek with the back of her fingers.

"And brought sunshine back into it," he said, taking Cassandra in his arms and kissing her.

The two closed the shop door behind them and began the perilous descent through the ancient wood and down to the river. Within half an hour, they were back in the village.

"I parked my car in the twenty-first century as it attracted too much attention last time - when I parked it over there," Cassandra said, pointing across the river to Wales.

"They won't have ever seen a motorcar," that's why. "It's going to take another four years before Evelyn Ellis imports a Panhard et Levassor."

"Yes, well mine's a Fiat," Cassandra said. "Hey, that's also French!" she added.

The two walked down to the ferry where the ferryman, once again, gave Cassandra a look made up of equal parts suspicion and fear.

Chapter Eleven

"What's his problem? I've got Victorian clothes on today," Cassandra asked, leaning into Lucius in order she not be overheard.

"It's your face - I told you, he's a relative of the husband you had that murdered you a year ago."

"That's creepy," Cassandra said. "When you say it like that it makes me feel like I've come back from the dead."

The ferry bumped into the opposite bank and Cassandra and Lucius quickly disembarked.

"Lucius, what's wrong?" Cassandra asked, grabbing hold of his arm.

"We're leaving the nineteenth century – I'm getting older," he said, his hair beginning to grey and his skin to wrinkle.

"But you said that I had made you young again after I first saw you in the shop."

"I don't know," he wheezed. "I can't explain it - look at my hands!" he said looking at his wrinkled hands and the liver spots that now marked them.

"Go back! I'm only going for my pill – I'm sure I'll be safe. I don't want to lose you,"

Chapter Eleven

Cassandra said, tears filling her eyes as she embraced Lucius and held him close to her.

"Nor I, you," he replied, his back beginning to curve into the stoop of age.

"Let me help you," Cassandra said, taking him by the arm.

"I'm sure I'll be fine when I'm back over there," he said, nodding to the far bank.

Cassandra guided Lucius back to the ferry and watched as he returned to more than a century before the moment they had parted, breathing a sigh of relief as his back straightened and his hair returned to black.

"I love you," she shouted, waving goodbye.

"Love you, too," Lucius replied, much to the scorn of a few passing dockers.

Cassandra made her way back to her car and changed back into modern attire. All the while she thought about how should she want to stay with Lucius, she would have to find the courage to say goodbye to the twenty-first century and her own time.

The drive back to the house she had shared with Simeon seemed to last an eternity before she drove into the street in which she had once lived,

Chapter Eleven

her heart pounding when she saw that Simeon's car was parked outside their former home.

Leaving her car unlocked, she quietly trod the path to the front door, annoyed that she would now only have a little time to pick up a few things and not have the time to change her passwords to keep Simeone from posting malicious things on her accounts.

Chapter Twelve

Cassandra tried to open the door as quietly as she could and, at first, assumed she had been successful.

"Who's there?" Simeon shouted from the living room. "Oh, it's you," he added, now that he stood by the living room door. "I knew you'd come crawling back to me once you had come to your senses," as his lips twisted into a cross between a smile and a sneer.

"I haven't, I've just come back to pick up a few things," Cassandra said, smiling a triumphant smile back at him.

"What?" he replied angrily, the smile on his face quickly dissolving into a look of fury.

Cassandra moved to the bottom of the stairs and quickly climbed them before hearing Simeon's phone ringing.

"I can't talk, mate – the bitch is back," she heard him say. "I'll call you later."

Cassandra grabbed a few things and thrust them into a holdall. Suddenly, she was aware that Simeon stood on the landing, gazing at her through the open bedroom door.

Chapter Twelve

"You can't leave me – we had a good thing going on," he said, taking a step nearer and blocking the doorway.

Without looking up, Cassandra continued packing, going back to her wardrobe for a few more things before responding.

"I've already left you - I've just returned for a few things. I'll soon be out of what's left of your hair," she said, looking at Simeon over her shoulder.

"Oh, yeah? You're not going anywhere - I won't let you. No one other than me would put up with your shit," he said.

"Fuck you," Cassandra replied. "No one tells me what to do," she hissed as she ducked underneath Simeon's arm now that he was attempting to block her exit by blocking the door with his hefty body, his right shoulder pressed against one side of the door frame and with his left arm outstretched, the palm of his hand pressed against the other side of the door frame.

As Cassandra passed him, he grabbed her arm, spinning her around and trying to force his open mouth onto her lips.

"No!" she said, pulling free of his grasp.

Chapter Twelve

"We were made for each other," he protested. "I won't let you go," he added as Cassandra turned away from him and ran down the stairs. Quickly opening the door, within a few moments she was back in her car. Turning the key, only to hear the engine making nothing but a click.

"No, don't do this," she shouted, looking up to see Simeon running down the garden path toward her. Within a second, his hand was on the handle of the door on her side of the car. He tried to open it but anticipating such a course of action Cassandra had already locked it. In his unabated fury, he began punching the door's window.

Again, Cassandra tried to start the car and this time the engine roared into life. Slamming the car into reverse, she sped away from the house.

Cassandra drove through the narrow lanes back to Lucius at speed, glancing in her rear-view mirror every few seconds to make sure Simeon wasn't following her and hoping that he would let her leave in peace.

Parking where her car had been parked less than an hour before, she quickly made her way back to the ferry, forgetting to change into her Victorian attire.

Chapter Twelve

"Yes? What's your fucking problem?" she shouted, as the ferryman approached and he began eyeing her with even more suspicion than he had when she had taken the route earlier that morning.

"Nothing," the man said, shaking his head and looking at the river.

"Then take me over there," she said, before pointing at the opposite bank and jumping on board.

A few minutes later she was back in the little village and the nineteenth century.

Lucius appeared, and ran toward her, rejuvenated, and vivified at having left the twenty-first century.

"Let's go for a drink," said Cassandra, closing her eyes in the warmth and security of his embrace.

"And you'd better get changed," he said, aware of the commotion Cassandra's modern attire would cause them and which were also causing a few glances.

"Why?" she asked.

"They've never seen a woman in trousers," he explained.

Chapter Twelve

"Oh God, really? I will get changed, as I've had enough of today, but I won't kowtow to what others expect of me. If they don't like me as I am then they can kiss my arse."

One drink later, and with Cassandra having changed into her Victorian clothes in the pub's toilets, they emerged and began to make their way down to the riverbank and back to the shop.

"Oh, shit, it's Simeon," Cassandra said, noticing a man crossing the river aboard the little ferry, his modern clothes causing as much interest as Cassandra's modern clothes had caused. "I don't think he recognises me in these clothes – it must be the hat," she added.

"Then act as if you don't know him. We shall deal with this when I've had time to think," Lucius said, taking hold of Cassandra's hand.

"I don't want the doorway to the nineteenth century to close and him and me to be both stuck here," Cassandra said to Lucius, trying to smile in the hope that what she was saying would be construed as something trivial.

As Lucius and Cassandra drew nearer to where the ferry had docked, Lucius leaned into Cassandra to speak to her.

Chapter Twelve

"I didn't have much of a look of him that first day you came to shop but now that I have ..."

"What? What is it?" Cassandra said, breathing a sigh of relief as Simeon walked past them.

"Cassandra, he was your husband – the man that killed you."

Chapter Thirteen

Cassandra fell mute at the thought that someone that had once taken her life was now stalking her. Worse still, she had been a partner of his in twenty-first-century life. Almost paralysed with fear, it took Lucius to break the evil spell Simeon's presence had wrought upon her.

"We need to get back to the shop," he said. "I have a few ideas."

Cassandra felt too scared to talk for most of the walk back to the shop, turning every few seconds to make sure they weren't being followed. Finally, they made it home.

"Back home," Lucius said, as they reached the cottage, Lucius reaching inside his coat pocket for his keys.

"At last," Cassandra said, breathing a sigh of relief that she had reached what already felt to her to be her sanctuary.

"We'll work this out, I promise. We're going to face this together," Lucius said.

"Kiss me," Cassandra asked, putting her hands on Lucius' shoulders, and tears filling her

Chapter Thirteen

eyes as she kissed him. "I knew something would spoil it," she added.

"We won't let it," Lucius said, opening the door so that they could both walk inside and leave the world behind them.

Cassandra let out a sigh.

"Ah, I feel safe here - in this little cottage," Cassandra said, breathing a second sigh of relief. "Now I can talk again without having to look over my shoulder."

"So, we have a problem," Lucius said, as he locked the door and walked across the shop toward the velvet curtain that separated the rooms. "We don't yet know why he's here, nor do we know his motives. He is the latest incarnation of the man that killed you last year but even though only a year has passed since then, he's slipped into what you and he think of as the past and so despite being born a century after he killed you, he appears to be the same age as he was when he did it."

"It disgusts me that I didn't recognise him when I met him in the twenty-first century - and, worse still, slept with him. He's a cruel bastard," Cassandra said, dabbing her eyes with a tissue.

Chapter Thirteen

"From what you told me last year, he always was. When you and I were lovers and he was your husband, he had a reputation for violence. The trouble is, he's a coward and only picked on those he thought wouldn't fight back – women, children, and cripples. This village was – and is – a rough and lawless area that attracted many people that we might think of as outsiders. He quickly found out that there were people here that made a living from fighting and that he was no match for them."

"So, how did we – you and me, I mean, not him and me - meet?" Cassandra asked, sitting down at the table as Lucius poured them a drink.

"You came to me one day after he had hit you. You needed a salve for the bruises and the pain. As I have said to you, souls recognise one another and I knew as soon as I saw you that you were the one I had loved and lost in the French Revolution, a century before," Lucius said, handing Cassandra a glass of wine.

Suddenly, the noise of the shop door opening interrupted them.

Chapter Thirteen

"Hold on," Lucius said, quickly rising to his feet. Brushing aside the velvet curtain, he entered the shop.

"Where's the old man?" Simeon asked, looking around the shop.

"Old man?" Lucius asked.

"Yes - I was here last week with the Missus and she said she'd seen an old man with white hair here. She's been visiting him since and I want to speak to him," Simeon said, the quiet fury in his voice tempered only by the fact that Lucius was more toned and muscular than him.

"There's no old man with white hair here, I assure you," Lucius said.

Cassandra quietly rose to her feet and moved to the velvet curtain to better hear the conversation about her.

"The lying bitch!" Simeon said. "I can't believe a word she says."

"Is there something else with which I can help you?" Lucius asked, parting his arms, and gesturing around the shop with open palms.

"No. Is this village being used for a film or something? Everyone's in fancy dress."

Chapter Thirteen

"No, this is how we live. Is there anything else?" Lucius replied his voice calm after a thousand years of experience in dealing with objectionable people.

"I suppose not," Simeon asked, looking around the shop in disgust. "Is there a McDonald's anywhere near here? I'm starving."

"McDonald's?" Lucius asked. "There's a James McDonald in the village," he added, moving to the shop's door, opening it, then standing next to it and smiling at Simeon.

"What are you on, mate?" Simeon asked as he walked past.

"Floorboards, I believe," Lucius said, looking at the floor, before closing the door behind Simeon.

Lucius watched as Simeon stood outside for a few moments, apparently perplexed, and looking at the cottage in confusion, his simple brain trying to make sense of why the shop looked in a state of good repair today compared to the abandoned and overgrown state in which he had seen it the week before. Pulling the map that his father had given him from his pocket when he and Cassandra had first used it to find the place, there

Chapter Thirteen

appeared to be a moment's elucidation on his face as he strode back down the woodland path.

"Thanks for that," said Cassandra, walking quietly across the shop floor to kiss Lucian's cheek and enjoy the sight of Simeon leaving them. "I'm glad he's gone. Do you think he'll be back?"

"I don't know. If he thinks you've lied to him then he's not going to have any idea where you are and that you might have said you were here but might be anywhere in the country. On the other hand, if he thinks you've left him for the man you told him about last week then he may return. He's a coward and a bully, so if he thinks there's an old man here that he can push around then he may return. Let's worry about that when – if – it happens, shall we?" Lucius said, returning Cassandra's kiss with a kiss of his own.

"I love how you take control of situations," she said. "Nothing seems to bother you."

"Thank you, but there are things that bother me," Lucius said.

"Such as?" Cassandra said, hoping such a fear was something she could assuage.

Chapter Thirteen

"Loneliness – and losing you," Lucius said, holding Cassandra close and kissing the tip of her nose.

The two of them spend the rest of that day, Lucius in his working apron preparing a few perfumes and Cassandra sat in the garden, enjoying the sunshine and birdsong, her mind on Simeon and whether or not he would attempt to spoil her happiness.

Chapter Fourteen

After an evening meal and a few more glasses of wine, the cares of the day seemed a distant memory.

"I've never wanted anyone more than you," Cassandra said, as the two lovers sat on high-backed chairs, facing one another. "Did you know we'd end up as lovers again when you told my fortune?"

"It wasn't a certainty, no. Life deals us a hand of cards but it is up to us how we play those cards," Lucius said, looking at Cassandra across the warm glow of the candles he had lit for them as day turned to night.

"I can see why in every life I've had, I've fallen for you," Cassandra said, smiling the smile of true affection at Lucius. "I've never met anyone else like you."

"And I've never wanted anyone but you," he replied, rising from his seat and walking around the table to kiss her, brushing her long hair from her face so that he could more easily see her expression.

"You're so beautiful," he said, leaning in for yet another kiss.

Chapter Fourteen

"Let's go to bed," she said, blowing out all but one of the candles, their flames dying until the room was finally illuminated less by candlelight and more by the pale light of the full moon as it cascaded through the leaded window.

In the bedroom, Cassandra lit a few candles from the one she had brought up the stairs with them and began to undress.

"Here, let me help you," Lucius said, standing behind Cassandra and unbuttoning her shirt, the two of them watching their reflections in a large mirror that stood in the corner of the room. As Cassandra's shirt fell to the floor, leaving her topless, Lucius cupped her pert breasts in his hand kissed her neck. Cassandra closed her eyes and sighed with pleasure before reaching behind her and stroking Lucius' groin, once again giggling with delight as it began to stiffen beneath her fingers.

"They're not too small for you are they, Lucius?" she asked, placing her hands on top of his.

"No, they're perfect."

"Here, let me undress you," Cassandra said, turning and unbuttoning Lucius' shirt and letting

Chapter Fourteen

it fall to the ground in a discarded heap, as they had with her shirt.

Seductively, Cassandra tugged at the buttons on his trousers, looking up at him through her long, dark eyelashes and then back down at her the light work her nimble fingers were making of unsheathing her lover.

"So big - so hard," she chuckled, kissing him and gently masturbating him after pulling his erection from his britches.

Cassandra sank to her knees, and took his virile member in her mouth, slipping it in and out as she moved her head back and forth.

"God, I've missed you," Lucius said, holding the back of her head, the pleasure causing his hands to tighten around a bunch of hair.

"Oh, I like that," Cassandra said. "Pull it harder."

Lucius did as he was requested, gasping for breath as pleasure ran through him like a torrent.

"What was that?" Cassandra said, startled by a noise outside.

"I didn't hear anything," Lucius said. "We're in the middle of a wood so it could be a badger or a fox."

Chapter Fourteen

"Okay, sweetheart," Cassandra said, her delicate hands taking a hold of Lucius' bare buttocks to slowly rock him back and forth into her mouth as she looked up at him cat-eyed, her dark pupils glimmering in the candlelight.

After a few minutes of fellatio, Cassandra paused and again looked up at Lucius, her eyes looking more like those of a feline than ever.

"That wine has gone to my head, Lucius. I'm so wet," she whispered. "Want to feel? Or fuck me?" she added, touching her most intimate part and then bringing the finger to her mouth to lick it as she arched an eyebrow and then winked at Lucius.

"I'd be delighted," Lucius said, helping Cassandra to her feet and carrying her to the bed.

"I want to see your face this time," she said, lying on her back and opening her legs as Lucius kneeled between her open thighs, slowly drawing his hand up and down his erection.

"I love watching you masturbate," Cassandra said. "Do you like watching me when I do it?" Cassandra asked, licking the finger on her right hand a second time before spreading her labia with a pair of fingers on her left hand.

Chapter Fourteen

"I also love watching you do it," Lucius said.

"Are you sure?" she teased, toying with her clitoris with the finger she had just moistened.

"More than you know," Lucius said.

"Fuck me," Cassandra said. "I need to feel you inside me."

Lucius rubbed the head of his swollen member up and down Cassandra's lips and then with one gentle push, slid himself inside her.

"Oh God, that feels so nice!" Cassandra said as Lucius ground against her, his pelvis pounding into the pelvis of his lover.

With one hand, he squeezed one of her erect nipples before taking it in his mouth and flicking his tongue all around her dark areola.

Each thrust brought him closer to orgasm but Cassandra, still rubbing her clitoris, was also close to a climax.

Lucius reached his hands underneath Cassandra, and squeezed her bare backside and feeling his erection slipping in and out, looking at Cassandra's beautiful face for signs of the pleasure he was bringing her.

Chapter Fourteen

"What is it?" she asked, after opening her eyes for a second and seeing that Lucius was looking at her.

"Nothing's the matter," he gasped. "I just love looking at you, seeing the pleasure on your face."

"I'm cumming," she said, bucking against Lucius' thrusts.

"Me too, he said," kissing her as he ejaculated deep inside her.

A few minutes passed as each lover caressed the other, exhausted in passion.

"Wow, that was amazing," Cassandra said, as Lucius rolled off, his chest heaving from the exertion.

"Incredible," he agreed, touching her face, and gazing lovingly into her eyes.

Just a few minutes later there was another noise outside.

"There's definitely something out there," Cassandra said.

"Yes, I heard it that time," Lucius said, moving to the window. "I can't see anything," after gazing into the darkness. "I'll take a look tomorrow."

Chapter Fifteen

The rest of that night was spent in a satiated stupor, each lover just a touch away from the other, their limbs often entwined as they enjoyed the sleep only lovers can know.

The next morning, Cassandra awoke to see Lucius at the window.

"What is it, sweetheart?"

"There's a ladder up against the tree outside our window," he answered. "It's one of mine, but I didn't put it there."

"Was it there yesterday?" Cassandra asked, sitting up in bed and pulling the sheets around her, as though the thin fabric might afford her some protection.

"No, it wasn't," Lucius said, turning from the window and looking at Cassandra with a steely expression on his face. "That must have been what we heard," he added.

"Oh, shit - I bet it was that bastard, back again," Cassandra said.

"Well, if it was, he seems to have taken what he saw quite well," Lucius said.

"You mean last night?" Cassandra asked.

Chapter Fifteen

"Yes, after all, I don't know how I would feel if I saw you doing what we did last night with another man."

"Would you be jealous?" Cassandra asked, looking around the bedroom for her clothes.

"More than jealous," Lucius said. "I'd want to kill him."

"He's too cowardly for that," Cassandra said. "As you said, people like him only hit people they know can't – or won't – fight back."

"Time will tell, but I'm ready for him," Lucius said, sitting on the edge of the bed to pull on his trousers.

"Maybe that will be the end of it and he'll go back to the twenty-first century."

"Perhaps," Lucius said.

"You don't sound very sure," Cassandra asked, suddenly feeling as if Lucius was keeping something from her.

"It's nothing," he replied, tying up his bootlaces.

"Do you know something? Have you seen something in the cards?"

Chapter Fifteen

"Not in the cards, no," tossing a pair of braces over his shoulder and fastening them to his trousers.

"Then where? Lucius, tell me," Cassandra demanded, more out of concern for Lucius than curiosity.

"I used a Ouija board while you were away to contact a spirit who's helped me since the twelfth century. I think the noise we heard last night *was* your ex."

"Oh, shit," Cassandra said, as she found her clothes and began getting dressed. "I hope he enjoyed the show, the pervert."

"Not as much as I did," Lucius said, slapping one of Cassandra's bare buttocks and leaning into her to kiss her.

"Nor me!" Cassandra said, as Lucius blew her a kiss from the bedroom door and descended the stairs, the moment of tension seeming to have passed.

As Lucius unlocked his shop, Simeon was waiting for him.

"Where is she? I'd like to speak to her," he demanded.

"Who?" Lucius asked.

Chapter Fifteen

"Look, mate, I know what's going on between you and her," Simeon replied.

"Oh, you do, do you?" said Lucius, folding his arms.

"Yes. I saw you both - last night. I have it all on here," Lucius said, pulling his mobile phone from his pocket. By now, the sun was warming the shop and the smell of the various perfumes that Lucius had created were becoming heady and intoxicating.

"What's that stink?" Simeon asked. "It smells like a brothel in here."

"Well, you'd know," said Cassandra, holding aside the velvet curtains that separated the rooms. Neither Lucius nor Simeon had heard her bare feet on the shop's floorboards and both turned around a little startled at hearing her speak.

"I saw you both - last night. I have it all on here," Lucius said.

"All what, exactly?" asked Cassandra.

"You two - last night. I saw him screwing you and you sucking his cock. It's all on here," Simeon said, waving his phone at Cassandra.

Chapter Fifteen

"So, what if it is," Cassandra replied. "It's all over between you and me. I can do what I want, when I want, with whomsoever I wish – I don't need your permission."

"Says who? If you don't come back to me, then I'm going to send this to everyone you know," Simeon glowered, tapping his right index finger against the phone he held in his left hand.

"Everyone?" Cassandra asked. "Such as who?" she added, trying to remain calm. "My parents are dead, I've no job and only one friend," she said, then paused. "Do you really think that trying to blackmail me into coming back to you is going to work?"

"I'll post it online," Simeon said, shaking his head in disgust.

"And say what? That your ex-partner is cheating on you? I wasn't cheating on you - I told you, it's over."

"You won't be quite so cocky when all the world sees you," Simeon said.

"That will be a century from now, so I shall be long gone."

"What sort of bollocks are you talking now?" Simeon asked, turning to Lucius. "Take it from me, mate - don't believe a thing this woman says," he said to Lucius, pointing at Cassandra in disgust.

"Then why do you want her back?" asked Lucius.

"Why don't you post it!" Cassandra asked, calling Lucian's bluff. "This is the year eighteen ninety-one. You can't hurt me or publicly humiliate me as the time you want to post it is over a century from now," said Cassandra.

"Ah, fuck it," Simeon said, kicking one of the display cabinets before turning and walking from the shop, slamming its door behind him.

"I knew he'd be like this," Cassandra said, watching as Simeon kicked open the gate that led from the property into the dark woodland.

"What's he doing?" Lucius asked, squinting as if looking at Simeon's back was the only way to figure out the machinations of the feeble-minded.

"He's trying to get a connection on his phone! Yeah, good luck with that," she added, as Simeon stomped off into the dense wood.

"I believe that this can now go one of two ways," Lucius said. "He can either catch the ferry back to his car, the twenty-first century and then

Chapter Fifteen

go back home without a problem," he paused. "Or he will start to age as the ferry crosses the river."

"How come I don't age when I cross it?" Cassandra asked.

"Every time is different and each time it's a gamble. It's not a dangerous gamble as all anyone needs to do is catch the ferry back and the process of ageing will reverse," Lucius explained.

"But if he can't get back to the modern age then he's stuck here - with us," Cassandra said, the horror of not being able to escape from Simeon having just occurred to her.

"Let's just see, shall we?" Lucius said. "If he can get back home, he's going to have a gadget that's been around for over a century so I don't think it's going to be something that will still work."

"I hadn't thought of that," Cassandra replied. "Sometimes technology letting us down is a blessing in disguise."

Meanwhile, on the riverbank, Simeon was making his way back to the village. "Bitch," he said to himself. Turning, he screamed it at the woodland he'd just left.

Chapter Fifteen

As Simeon arrived in the village, the ferry was just about to disembark.

"Hold on!" he shouted, jumping on board.

"I know you," said the ferryman. "You look just like the cousin of the other fella that usually does this job."

"Handsome, is he?" Simeon asked, puffing up his chest in conceit.

"Dead," said the ferryman. "They hung him last year for killing his wife."

"I don't blame him – she probably deserved it," Simeon replied, beginning to wince in pain as the ferry moved across the river.

"You alright?" asked the ferryman.

"No, do I look alright? My knees and back are killing me."

"It's not that, it's your hair and face."

"What's wrong with them?" Simeon asked, pulling his phone from his pocket, and taking a selfie. "Shit, what's happening to me?" he said in astonishment as he saw a photo of what appeared to be the face of an old man staring out from the phone's tiny screen.

"Your hair is falling out and your face has aged about fifty years in two minutes," the

Chapter Fifteen

ferryman said, pointing at the hair on Simeon's hoody and then to the hair on the floor.

"I can see that," Simeon said, rolling his eyes as if the ferryman's observation was obvious.

"Just saying," said the ferryman, his grimy face breaking into a leer. "You're still a nice-looking fella, though."

"I think I need a doctor – are there any in the village?" Simeon asked.

"Yes, there's one up that lane," said the ferryman, pointing back into the village. "If it's the clap you've got, then he's your man."

"Take me back," Simeon begged, grabbing a hold of the ferryman's arm.

"We need to get to the other bank, first. You're not the only one on board," the ferryman replied, pulling his arm free.

By now, Simeon was doubled over and losing his teeth. He sat down as the ferry landed and waited for it to make its return journey.

As the ferry's passengers climbed aboard and it started making its way back, Lucius looked at his hands. They were gnarled, wrinkled, spattered with liver spots, and had cracked and broken nails. As the ferry made its slow approach

Chapter Fifteen

back to the village, the wrinkles began to disappear. By the time they had reached the bank on the English side of the Wye, Simeon was able to stand upright.

"Don't know what happened there," he said to the ferryman.

"Just a funny turn, I s'pose," the ferryman replied.

Chapter Sixteen

The day was a very warm one and feeling a little more confident that Simeon may have returned to the twenty-first century with a broken phone, Cassandra suggested that Lucius leave the shop door open to let in a breeze.

"*Oui, Mademoiselle*," he said.

"Oh, stop it! You've never seen *The Addams Family*, have you? I never understood how hearing Morticia speak French could have such an effect on Gomez until I heard you!" said Cassandra.

"No, I've never seen them. Are they friends of yours?" asked Lucius.

"No, it's an old TV show."

"TV? What's that?" Lucius asked.

"It doesn't matter. It's a box that sits in the corner of the room that shows moving images."

"Sounds a bit boring, no?"

"*Oui*, most definitely *oui*, but that show was a great one."

Lucius pottered about his shop, making scents that nobody would ever buy and Cassandra, to keep him company, polished the wooden shelves and worktops.

Chapter Sixteen

"So, we first met two centuries ago in Paris?" she asked.

"Yes - although the days between then and now seem to have disappeared," Lucius replied, stopping for a moment to stare wistfully into the distance.

"And I was a courtesan?"

"Yes, you were, although after we met you gave up the profession. I think poverty drove you to it."

"I was poor?"

"Yes, a lot of people in Paris at that time were desperately poor," Lucius replied.

"Yes, I remember from school that revolutionaries used the phrase 'let them eat cake' to attack the aristocracy of the *Ancien Régime,* as it was a quote attributed to one of the ruling elite."

"And losing you is a tragedy that has haunted me for centuries. I have lost count of the times I have asked myself if having taken you out of poverty, is it my fault that you were then mistaken for a member of the aristocracy and killed by members of the *Montagnards*."

"Did you hear something?" Cassandra said, pointing to the open door and placing her index

Chapter Sixteen

finger to her mouth to gesture for Lucius to be quiet.

"No - what was it?" he asked.

"I thought I heard footsteps," Cassandra replied.

"Maybe you're still a little worried about what happened earlier."

"Maybe," Cassandra replied, falling silent for a minute but after hearing no further noise, she continued.

"So, I was a prostitute and then, later, my husband attacked me for having an affair with you and was hung for it?"

"Yes, that's right," Lucius said.

"I knew it!" Simeon said, stepping in through the open door.

"God, you made me jump," Cassandra said, holding her chest and taking a few steps backwards. "Knew what?"

"That you had a past. Didn't mention online that you'd been a hooker or that you'd been married and had an affair with him," Simeon said, pointing at Lucius.

"So, you only heard the last sentence, did you?"

Chapter Sixteen

"For fuck's sake, don't tell me there's more!" Lucius said in disbelief.

"All you heard was me saying that I'd once been a prostitute and that my husband had attacked me for having an affair with Lucius."

"Who's Lucius?" shouted Simeon.

"He's Lucius," Cassandra replied, pointing at Lucius as he replaced his pestle in its mortar and fixed his gaze on Simeon.

"How much of this was going on behind my back?" Simeon raged.

"None of it."

"Why are you lying? I just heard you say it and now you know that I heard you you're denying having said it!"

"What you didn't hear me saying was that I'd been a prostitute two centuries ago and that I was reincarnated to a life here and despite being married to a previous incarnation of you, I fell in love with Lucius and when you found out you killed me. That was one hundred and thirty years ago. We have slipped back in time to a year after you killed me and that's why people in the village think that we're haunting them – they fished my body from the river after you hit my head with a

Chapter Sixteen

rock and threw me in the Wye. You were found guilty of murder and hung for it," Cassandra said, as if she were talking to an errant child.

"Do you believe this crap?" Simeon said, wrinkling his nose as if he'd just smelt a noxious smell, and addressing his question to Lucius. "We're going home," he said, grabbing Cassandra by her wrist and dragging her to the door.

"Don't touch me, you bastard," Cassandra said, struggling to free herself as she punched Simeon in the back and kicked his legs.

"Get your hands off her," Lucius said, blocking the door. Neither Cassandra nor Simeon had seen or heard him move and the demand so struck fear into the immortal soul of the cowardly Simeon that he let loose Cassandra's wrist.

"Look, mate, I'm doing you a favour! You should be paying me for taking her off your hands," Simeon protested, throwing open his arms and looking at Lucius.

"Cassandra has made it very clear that she doesn't want to leave with you," Lucius said. "Until such a time as she says otherwise, there's nothing here for you."

Chapter Sixteen

"Well, that's it then," Simeon said. "If you're not coming back with me then I may as well end it all," Simeon said, looking back at Cassandra. "And it will all be your fault," he added.

"Oh, that's ridiculous. When you had me, you were vile and told me that you were only with me until someone better came along - now you've lost me you can't live without me!"

"Yes, make fun all you like but I loved you," Simeon said, wiping his eyes in the hope Cassandra would think he was crying. "I'm going," he said, walking past Lucius and leaving the two lovers behind him.

Chapter Seventeen

Lucius closed the shop door and took Cassandra in his arms, tenderly pressing his lips against her forehead. Tears began to stream down Cassandra's face.

"I'm sorry you have to go through this," Lucius whispered.

"I'm not crying because of him, I'm crying because of you," Cassandra replied.

"Me?" Lucius said, surprised at hearing the words.

"Yes. I've had three lifetimes of dealing with people like him but you're the only man to ever show me any kindness - and that's why I'm crying," she tearfully whispered.

"Oh, Cassandra," Lucius said, pressing his lips to her forehead a second time. "Whatever happens *we* will deal with it," Lucius said, then paused. "We're a team, so even if it's us versus the world, it will still be *us* versus the world, not *you* versus the world."

On hearing the words, Cassandra began to sob.

"I love you," she murmured.

"And I love you, too," Lucius replied.

Chapter Seventeen

"I don't know how long we've been stood like this but it's over an hour since I last looked at the clock when Simeon left," Cassandra.

"It's one of life's cruel jokes that a moment spent in paradise passes as quickly as a month in hell," Lucius replied.

"Lucius, I need to make one last return to the twenty-first century. I've made up my mind that I want to stay here with you but I should tell my friend Anna as she may be worried about me if I just disappear. She'd never met Simeon but I'd told her about him and how unhappy I was with him," she said, looking at Lucius and stroking his cheek with loving affection. "If I just disappear, she may think that he's done something to me."

"You do whatever you need to do, sweetheart," Lucius replied, rubbing his hand up and down her back, through the fabric of her dress.

"Right, I shan't be long," Cassandra said, giving Lucius a quick kiss and walking from the room and back to the bedroom to fetch her car keys. When she returned, Lucius was donning his work apron.

Chapter Seventeen

"I shall see you later," Cassandra said, blowing Lucius a kiss as she stood by the shop door.

The journey down the steep path now seemed less arduous than it had when first she had climbed it. Maybe she was getting used to it or becoming a little more fit with the exercise after being housebound for a year due to the pandemic lockdown.

As she walked alongside the river, her mind was on Lucius and the joy he had brought her. Before long she was back in the village. Dockers were already working on the river, loading barges with logs from the Forest of Dean. Thankfully, the ferryman that recognised was not working that day and so she was able to travel across the river without issue. A few passengers seemed to look at her askance, as if recognising her as the woman that had been murdered the year before but, Cassandra told herself, they might just be thinking that she looked a little like that woman and that maybe that woman had a sister.

Back at her car, Cassandra quickly changed into her modern clothes. Thankfully, the car started and as she had not parked it in the

Chapter Seventeen

nineteenth century the fate Lucius had predicted would befall Lucius' phone had not befallen her car.

The drive back through the Wye Valley was as beautiful as always, past cliffs and views down the Severn Estuary. Soon she was parking her car outside Anna's house.

Cassandra locked her car and walked the path to Anna's door. Anna hadn't been expecting her but that would be fine as she knew Anna was always pleased to see her.

Cassandra rang the doorbell and soon after Anna answered the door.

"Cass! Where've you been? I've been thinking about you," Anna said, giving Cassandra a hug and holding the door open so that Cassandra could enter.

"Wow, do I have a tale to tell you!" Cassandra said, following Anna to her kitchen.

"Coffee?" Anna asked.

"Yes, please – no milk."

"So, what's this story?" Anna asked as she waited for the kettle to boil.

"Remember when I was last here?"

Chapter Seventeen

"Do I ever!" Anna said, batting her eyelashes.

"And me saying that I wanted to be seduced?" Cassandra said, smiling and rubbing her friend's arm.

"I did my best, Cass," Anna laughed.

"Well, I went for that day out with Simeon, the following day, as planned, and we found this old place covered in ivy. It looked like a ruin but it was a shop – an apothecary shop – that hadn't had a customer in fifty years! We went in, and the shopkeeper was still there. The idiot didn't see him but I saw him. After we got home, dickhead and I started arguing and, I swear, I almost stuck a knife in him."

"Cass, you need to be careful! That temper of yours is going to get you into trouble," Anna said, surprised but not shocked as she knew what her friend was like when her temper was roused and that she had never been one to cut fools much slack.

"It's fine, I didn't do it," Cassandra replied, flicking her hair over her shoulders. "Anyway, I went back to the shop the next day, on my own,

Chapter Seventeen

and the man that lived in the shop read my tarot cards."

"Ooh, that sounds interesting. I'd love to have someone read mine," Anna said, heaping coffee into two mugs and pouring boiling water into them. "Did he forecast a lover for you?"

"I'm coming to that," Cassandra said, widening her eyes and nodding. "Well, I went back the day after he'd read my cards, and the old man I'd seen the day before had turned into a young man as I'd gone back to the nineteenth century!"

"What?" Anna said, almost dropping her teaspoon.

"Yes, I've spent the last week in eighteen ninety-one, with a man born in the eleventh century!" Cassandra replied, hoping her friend would share in her excitement.

"Cass, let's sit down," Anna said, drawing a chair away from her kitchen table for Cassandra to sit, then pulling a second chair from the table to sit in front of her friend. "Don't be offended, but this sounds a little bit …" Anna added, struggling to find the right word, lest the wrong word cause offence.

Chapter Seventeen

"And he told me that I used to be a courtesan in the eighteenth century and that in a later life he and I became lovers again but that I was murdered a year before I met him," Cassandra said, taking a sip of coffee.

"Cass, you and I are old friends," Anna began, "but this sounds crazy."

"I know! That cosmic ordering thing you suggested – where I had to ask the universe for what I wanted and I asked to be seduced – really worked!" Cassandra replied, still oblivious to the fact that her friend didn't believe her.

"And what does Simeon have to say about this?" Anna asked, leaning back in her chair, and rubbing her hands on the back of her head.

"He doesn't like it but now he's trapped there in the same year as me and I think he may be dead."

"Dead!"

"Yes - even if he isn't, you won't be seeing him again."

"Again? I've never met him, remember?" Anna said, the veracity of her friend's strange tale sounding more far-fetched by the second.

Chapter Seventeen

"So, this is the third life I've had since I met Lucius," Cassandra said, clapping her hands together and smiling.

"Lucius?" queried Anna.

"Sorry, I forgot to mention his name. The man that read my cards and with whom I've been living in the nineteenth century is Lucius, d'Orsay – he's French. He used to be a knight, and was a member of the *Rose-Croix*."

"Okay, Cass. Have you ever thought about counselling? I know a lot of people have struggled under the lockdown but what you're saying does sound," again Anna struggled to be tactful. "Odd," she added.

"I thought you'd be pleased for me," Cassandra said, looking crestfallen.

"You had a brain tumour when you were younger, didn't you?"

"What's that got to do with it?" Cassandra asked, her eyes widening with surprise.

"I just wonder if counselling might help you," Anna said, stroking her friend's arm in pity. "Why don't you consider it?"

"You don't believe me, do you?" Cassandra said, putting down her mug on a coaster.

Chapter Seventeen

"I'm sure you believe it's true, Cass," Anna said, trying to sound sympathetic.

"It is true!"

"What does Simeon have to say about it?"

"Oh, bollocks to him. I've just told you, you won't be seeing him again," Cassandra said. "He's stuck in the nineteenth century and threatening to kill himself."

"What was his surname?" Anna asked, trying not to show that Cassandra's tale had given her such a cause for concern that she was worried about his wellbeing.

"His name is Simeon Danton. Why? Do you think I've made him up as well?" Cassandra said, folding her arms.

"I'm just asking, Cass. It's only a small town and neither Andy or I know of anyone named Simeon. Andy even looked up the name on Facebook and none of the people named Simeon that we found on there were saying they were in a relationship with you."

"Oh my God, you don't believe me!"

"Cass, calm down – please," Anna said.

"Don't tell me what to do," Cassandra said, beginning to feel angry with her friend.

Chapter Seventeen

"Cass, please."

"I thought you'd be pleased for me! I only came back to tell you that you won't be seeing me again as I'm going to live with Lucius in the nineteenth century. There's a chance the doorway between what we think of as that time and what we think of as today may close and so I won't be able to return – and, to be honest – I wish I hadn't bothered coming back today, now I know the reception that you've given me," Cassandra said, pausing for a moment. "I'm sick of the twenty-first century," she added.

"Well, I don't think many people are very happy at the moment, babe. We've all been shut inside for a year and it's causing us all a few problems," Anna said.

"Oh God, I'm telling you facts! I've not lost my mind, I assure you. You seem to think that the men in white coats need to come and take me away," Cassandra said, looking at the ceiling of Anna's kitchen as if seeking divine intervention.

"Cass, please think about counselling – I don't want you to do anything stupid," Anna said, reaching out a hand to her friend.

Chapter Seventeen

"Don't touch me! I thought I could tell you everything," Cassandra said, pushing her friend's hand away from her.

"You can, but I'm not a counsellor," Anna replied, trying her best to sound concerned but starting to feel a little scared that her friend had lost her mind after spending too long shut indoors.

"Look, when I had a brain tumour I was going back and forth to the doctors' for years and all I ever got was the same look of pity, disgust and impatience from them that I'm getting from you right now! Even after I collapsed and needed emergency surgery, not one of them apologised. As a matter of fact, I tried to explain to the neurosurgeon how ill I was feeling at the first consultation I had with him after the operation and all he did was look at his nails as I was talking to him and then tell me that the only thing that would help me would be fucking counselling!"

"How about mindfulness? That may help you," Anna persisted.

"Look, I have physiological damage," Cassandra said, letting out a sigh. "I've seen the scans so that's not me being a hypochondriac. It hasn't made me crazy, or prone to imagining things! What it has done, is caused nerve damage. How is counselling going to help with that! That's like saying to someone with a broken arm that you're not going to put it in a cast but have a chat about it! I did psychology as part of my degree so the last thing I need is someone telling me to pace myself, write lists, and practice mindfulness! If you had arthritis, do you think counselling would help you?"

"It may be an idea, Cass. After all, he knows best," Anna replied.

"Right, I'm going," Cassandra said, rising to her feet.

"Cass, where are you going?"

"Far away from here – to the past!" Cassandra replied, moving to Anna's front door.

"Cass, please come back. I will try to get you the help you need," Anna said looking around for her phone.

"Don't bother – I'm going. Goodbye," Cassandra said, opening the door and closing it firmly behind her.

"Hello, police please," Anna said, having finally found her phone and telephoned for help.

Chapter Seventeen

"I'm concerned about my friend. Yes, she's just been here and is saying some very odd things. I think she may either harm someone or harm herself. Her name is Cassandra Wyvern. Yes, I'd be happy to give you a statement."

"Unbelievable," Cassandra said, as she started her car. "Right, let's pick up a few things and get the hell out of here"

Cassandra then made her way back to the house she had once shared with Simeon.

"Ah, good! He's not here," she said to herself as she pulled up outside. "Time to pack a few suitcases. Twenty twenty-one can then kiss my ass goodbye!"

Chapter Eighteen

Cassandra finished packing her things and loaded them in her car. Looking around, she wondered if this would be the last time that she would ever see the modern-day.

The drive back to Lucius was a strange one as it had a finality to it and even though she was going to a place she hoped would be a happier one for her, she still felt like she was saying goodbye to an old friend.

She parked her car in Wales and changed her clothes. A car of young lads drove passed and one of them shouted a lecherous obscenity at her, throwing an empty cup from McDonald's at her, after seeing her removing her jeans.

"God, I won't be sorry to see the back of assholes like that," she said to herself.

As she waited on the riverbank, she breathed a sigh of relief to see that the ferryman on duty today was not the one that thought he recognised her.

On the far shore, she could see various labourers busying themselves loading a barge, smiling to herself that the streets, shops, and pub looked like something from a movie.

Chapter Eighteen

Then the thought that Simeon might still be in the village came back to her and her smile faded.

The walk back to the shop was one she should have enjoyed, given it was a new beginning for her but her suitcase was heavy and so the journey took even longer than usual. Every now and then, she turned her head to make sure she was not being followed.

She smiled as she passed the bushes where Lucius and she had shared a passionate moment in the waters of the Wye.

As she gazed up the steep path into the wood, she wondered why Lucius had ever thought that a shop so hidden from view would ever do well, even though the path was beautiful and reminded her of something from a fairy tale.

"Lucius," she shouted, as she drew near the cottage. There, in the garden, Lucius was sat in the sun, next to his sprawling, poisonous castor bean shrub.

"Ah, Cassandra," he said, rising to her feet and coming to greet her. "Let me help you," he added, taking the suitcase from her.

Chapter Eighteen

"Well, I'm back! Did you miss me?" she asked.

"Of course," he replied.

"I went to see my friend but wish I hadn't bothered," Cassandra said, as Lucius opened the shop door.

"Why, what happened?"

"I told her what had happened to me - that I'd met you and that you were born in the eleventh century, that we had met twice before in my past lives, and she didn't believe me."

"I suppose it does sound a bit far-fetched when you say it like that," he said, wrapping a comforting arm around her.

"And she told me I needed counselling – and that really pissed me off, as I almost died because doctors would only suggest counselling and wouldn't listen to me when I told them how ill I felt," she fumed.

"Come inside," Lucius said. "I'll pour us a drink and we can sit out here in the sun," he added, picking up Cassandra's case and carrying it into the shop.

"A drink would be wonderful," Cassandra said.

Chapter Eighteen

"Hold on," Lucius said, opening a door to his cellar and descending its worn, stone steps. "Here we are," he said, returning with a bottle of wine. "Here we have a Chateau Margaux, seventeen eighty-seven."

"As mentioned by Poe in his *Thou Art the Man*," Cassandra said.

Lucius uncorked the wine and held open the door for Cassandra to return to the garden.

"Please, sit down," he said, gesturing to his chair. "I shall go and get myself another one," he added, handing Cassandra his drink.

Cassandra sat down and waited for Lucius to return. A minute or two later, he returned with his chair.

"This wine is wonderful," Cassandra said.

"I thought you'd like it."

"I love it," she replied. "But you know how naughty I can get after a drink," she said, giving Lucius a wink.

"Shame on you, Miss Wyvern," Lucius said. "You don't need a drink to be naughty with me," he said, laughing.

Chapter Eighteen

"Lucius, I have to ask, why do you have so many poisonous plants in your garden? I know the castor bean is deadly," Cassandra said.

"I find them fascinating," Lucius replied. "Take this one - Brugmansia, or angel's trumpet, is a member of the same family as deadly nightshade," he said, gesturing to plant growing next to him. "It's an amazing aphrodisiac but can kill you if you take too much of it - but an amazing way to die as it's pain-free. Even the cuttings from a pruned laurel hedge can emit fumes so toxic that to breathe them risks one falling into unconsciousness."

Wide-eyed at why Lucius ad such an interest in deadly plants, Cassandra took another sip of wine and persisted with her question.

"So why do you grow so many deadly plants? You even have opium poppies!" Cassandra asked. "I'm curious."

Lucius laughed and took a large sip of wine.

"It's not that I poison people, or add any of them to any of my medications or perfumes."

"What is it, then?" Cassandra asked, her curiosity piqued by the apparent reluctance of Lucius to tell her.

Chapter Eighteen

"I don't need a memento mori to remind me that life is short as for me it is not," he said. "But these plants," he added, gesturing to the plants in his garden, "remind me that nature is in control. Man is a vain buffoon if he thinks he can tame such a force."

Chapter Nineteen

L ucius stood up and took Cassandra's hand, helping her to her feet. The two then walked the short distance from the lawn and back to the shop.

"What is it? What's wrong?" Cassandra asked.

"Nothing, it's just that sitting in the sun is making the wine go to my head," he answered.

"I logged on to the ex's computer while I was there, and he hasn't logged on since he followed me here."

"That's a good thing, no?" Lucius asked.

"Yes and no. It means he hasn't uploaded the video he took of us," said Cassandra, pausing for breath. "But it probably means he's still here - and that means that sooner or later he'll be back."

"He's been here while you were away," Lucius said.

"Oh no, why didn't you say? What did he want?" Cassandra replied, leaning her back against one of the shop counters.

"He said that he wanted you back and that he wanted to speak to you. I told him that you weren't here and had gone back to the twenty-first century but I don't think he believed me. He said

Chapter Nineteen

that when he'd tried to go back home, he had turned into an old man and couldn't even get off the ferry."

"How can we get rid of him? He's going to spoil everything," Cassandra said, lost in thought as she gazed at the sunshine streaming through the door, its rays like ghostly, gossamer fingers.

"He says that if you won't go back to him then he will kill himself," Lucius added,

"Well, that's up to him - I won't cave in to blackmail."

"No, and if he does kill himself then he has issues that go a lot deeper than you ending your relationship with him. Anyway," Lucius said, walking toward Cassandra who, by now, was sat on the shop counter, "we now have each other," he added, lifting her hands from her lap and kissing the backs of her fingers.

"Yes, we do," Cassandra said, placing her hands on Lucius' shoulders, pulling him toward her and kissing him. "And I'm feeling a bit tipsy – and you know what that means," she added, blowing him a kiss.

"Cassandra, I can't go on without you. You have to come back to me," said a voice from near

Chapter Nineteen

the door that startled both Cassandra and Lucius as neither had heard the owner of the voice approaching the shop. Both Cassandra and Lucius turned and there, staring at them, stood Simeon.

"No, Simeon, listen to me, "Cassandra said, getting down from the counter. "It's over between us - I love Lucius," she added, pointing at Lucius. "When we were together you were horrible to me. You only want me back now because you wanted to be the one to end it and it's too great a blow to your vanity and ego to have a woman finish with you."

"That's bullshit! Are you coming, or not?" Simeon asked.

"No, it's over."

"I can't even get back to the twenty-first century," he implored. "I'm stuck here – in a place I don't know, with people I don't know – and it's all your fault."

"I didn't ask you to follow me," Cassandra said, turning to Lucius in exasperation. "You always do, this," she added, looking back at Simeon.

"Do what?" he asked.

"Gaslight me."

Chapter Nineteen

"What? I don't know what you're talking about," Simeon said, a look of disgust on his face.

"Try and sow seeds of doubt in my mind and try and have me question my memory or judgement."

"That's bullshit," Simeon said, slowly walking back and forth, like a bored caged beast.

"You did it to make me feel as though I was to blame for your unhappiness and that I needed you for emotional support as you were the only one that I could trust. Well, you underestimated me for if it hadn't been a pandemic sweeping the country then I'd have left you months ago."

"I followed you here because I love you," Simeon said, taking a step nearer to her.

"No, you don't – you followed me here because you're a controlling narcissist with a fragile ego. I know what you're like - even if I did come back to you, you'd be horrible again within an hour."

"So, there's a chance then? Cass, I've changed."

"No, there's no chance. I want to stay here," she said. "With him" she added, pointing at Lucius who, while still standing nearby, had

Chapter Nineteen

stayed silent and let Cassandra and Simeon end their ties with one another themselves.

"Then screw you, you bitch," Simeon said, turning to leave.

"See, you haven't changed at all! Still throwing a tantrum because you can't have your way," Cassandra said, looking at Lucius and rolling her eyes.

Simeon didn't stop to listen and left, slamming the door behind him.

"Oh God, what did I ever see in that idiot!" she said.

"Twice," Lucius replied.

"Twice?" queried Cassandra.

"Yes – you were once married to him, remember?"

"Ah, yeah – and he murdered me," Cassandra said, the wheels turning in her mind as she now wondered whether history was once again going to repeat itself.

"Yes, he did."

"Do you think he'll try and do it again?" Cassandra asked.

"No, I don't think so. What's more, this time you don't live with him, you live with me," Lucius

Chapter Nineteen

said, stepping forward to wrap Cassandra in his arms.

"What do the cards say?" Cassandra asked.

"I don't know, I haven't looked. Shall we see?" Lucius asked.

"Yes," Cassandra said, breathing a sigh of relief. "Shall we have another drink?" she asked. "I need to get out of this room for a start and a drink will help take my mind off it. Can we lock up for the day?"

"Of course – anything for you, sweetheart," Lucius said, walking to the door and locking it. He then returned to Cassandra and ran his fingers through her hair as he looked lovingly at her face.

"I must have come back to you a third time as we have something unfinished," Cassandra said. "I don't want a tragedy to take me from you again."

"Neither do I," Lucius said, kissing her.

"My legs turn to jelly when you kiss me like that," she murmured, closing her eyes as Lucius kissed her again. "I wish we knew we had the day to ourselves," she added. "I need you inside me."

"Well, we can always forget about the cards," Lucius replied, holding the side of her face with the palm of his hand, and stroking her lips with his thumb."

"No, we need to know what's going to happen," Cassandra said, letting out a sigh.

"Your wish is my command, dear lady," Lucius said, following Cassandra as she walked toward the back room, pulled aside the velvet curtain, and entered. "Oh, I forgot your suitcase," he added, spinning on his heel, returning a moment later carrying it.

"Yes, we don't want to forget that," Cassandra said, suggestively.

"That sounds intriguing."

"Good," she replied, as Lucius fetched the pack of tarot cards.

"Would you like to shuffle them?" Lucius asked, handing Cassandra the cards, and sitting down opposite her.

"Yes, okay," she replied, shuffling them, then handing them back to Lucius.

"Now, choose three," he said, spreading them out onto the polished tabletop.

Cassandra leaned forward and pulled one from the pack.

Chapter Nineteen

"Ah, the lovers," she said, breathing a sigh of relief and blowing Lucius a kiss.

"Would you like to choose another?" he said, smiling and blowing a kiss back.

Cassandra reached forward and turned a second card.

"Oh no, not again!" she said, looking at The Hanged Man card. "That's all I need."

"It doesn't mean that anyone's going to hang themselves," Lucius said, reaching across the table to give Cassandra's hand a reassuring squeeze.

"No, but with some lunatic running around threatening to kill himself then it's not the card I wanted to see, even if I'm not to take it literally."

"Do you want to choose a third?" Lucius said, giving Cassandra's hand another reassuring squeeze.

"Oh, I don't believe it!" Cassandra said, turning the card over. "Death."

"It doesn't mean death as we think of it but the end of one chapter and a new beginning," Lucius said.

"I remember but, again, what if it does mean what it says?" Cassandra asked.

Chapter Nineteen

"If it does – and Simeon does choose to end his life here in the nineteenth century, then that will mean he will have died before he was ever born," Lucius said.

"I don't follow you – what does that mean?" said Cassandra, her brow knitting in confusion.

"It will mean that he was never born and so no trace of him will exist. He will disappear from the memory of everyone that ever knew him."

"No way! Really?" Cassandra said, her jaw dropping in disbelief.

"Yes - he will have died a century before he was ever born so people in his own time won't even know that such a man ever existed," Lucius said.

"Some people think I'm already crazy," Cassandra said, thinking of what Anna had said to her about her needing counselling. "If I start talking about someone that never existed, they're going to think I've lost it."

"No, they won't," Lucius said.

"You don't know my friends," Cassandra replied.

"You won't mention him."

Chapter Nineteen

"I might, if the memory of the way he treated me plays on my mind."

"It won't," Lucius said. "He will never have existed for everyone – including you."

"That's so bizarre," Cassandra said, shaking her head in disbelief. "There may be thousands of people out there that had relationships with people and those people somehow slipped back in time, died there, and so were never born – and the people they had relationships with now have no memory of them."

"Yes, that's true," Lucius said.

"So, how will I remember the year I spent with him?"

"You won't have spent it with him as he never existed," Lucius explained.

"So, I may have met someone else?"

"Yes."

"Hang on a minute – if I'd never have met him, I'd never have gone on that day out with him, never come here, and never met you," Cassandra said.

"You and I were destined to be together," Lucius said. "However difficult the circumstance, love would have overcome them."

Chapter Nineteen

"Are you sure?" Cassandra asked, breathing a sigh of relief.

"I promise," Lucius said.

"God, I want you," she said, standing and reaching out to take a hold of Lucius' hand.

Lucius stood and walked around the table, picking up Cassandra's suitcase.

"Then I suppose we'd better go upstairs," he said.

Lucius let Cassandra go in front of him and followed behind her with her suitcase. As soon as Cassandra entered the warm room she turned around and passionately kissed Lucius, running her hands through his hair to pull his head closer to hers.

Taking her hands from his hair, she slowly undid the buttons of his shirt until his chest was exposed. Kissing his neck, she crouched and looked up and him through her eyelashes as she licked his nipple, her left hand rubbing the growing bulge in the front of his trousers.

"Oh, Miss Wyvern, you have the most delicate touch," he said, groaning with pleasure.

Chapter Nineteen

Unbuttoning his trousers, she gently tugged them down before cupping his testes in her hand and giving them a rub.

"You like that?" she asked, as he groaned.

"Very much."

Sinking to her knees, she began to masturbate him, looking up at him to enjoy the pleasure on his face.

"Sit on the edge of the bed," she asked, removing his trousers, and tossing them to one side.

Lucius happily obliged, as Cassandra held his erection in one hand and looked up at him.

"Cass, that feels so nice," he said.

"I love licking your balls."

"And I love you licking them," he groaned.

Standing up, Cassandra quickly turned and hitched up her dress.

"No underwear!" Lucius said.

"I thought you'd like it," she said, sitting on his lap and wriggling as he reached around to massage her breasts through the thin fabric. "I've also brought something from the twenty-first century that may be fun.

"What's that, then?"

Chapter Nineteen

"It's in my suitcase - let me watch you play with yourself while I get it," she said, dashing to her suitcase and watching Lucius masturbate as he watched her.

"Here it is!" she said, holding a vibrator aloft.

"A dildo?" Lucius asked.

"No, a vibrator. I've always fantasised about having two men but I don't want to have sex with anyone but you. With this, you can use it on me and I can suck you and pretend both are you," she giggled, letting her dress fall to the floor.

"My God, I've missed you," Lucius said, still stroking his erection.

Within seconds, Cassandra was lying next to him on the bed.

"Want to see me play with it?" she teased.

"Yes, please!" he said, as Cassandra lay back on the bed and opened her legs. Switching the vibrator on, she began rubbing all around her groin, her free left hand massaging her left breast.

"Don't stop playing with yourself," she ordered. I want to put on a show for you – and know that it's turning you on so much you have to take yourself in hand!"

Chapter Nineteen

Moving her hand down her body, she parted her lips and began running the vibrator over her clitoris.

"Oh God," Lucius gasped.

"You like? Watch this," Cassandra said, bringing the vibrator to her mouth and sucking it. With the vibrator still wet, she quickly brought it down the bed. With two fingers on her left hand, she parted her lips and slid the vibrator inside herself.

"I have to lick you," Lucius said, leaning forward and licking Cassandra's clitoris.

"You can use it on me if you want. I want to suck you," she suggested, patting the bed for Lucius to lie next to her.

"Like this?" he asked, lying next to her.

"No, like this," Cassandra said, straddling his face with her open legs before bending forward and taking his penis into her mouth.

Lucius began licking Cassandra's clitoris as she performed oral sex on him, sometimes licking it, sometimes sucking it, sometimes running her lips up and down the shaft, sometimes taking it in her mouth and sliding it in and out of it.

Chapter Nineteen

Lucius slid the vibrator deep inside his lover, all the while licking her and savouring the taste.

"If you keep doing that, Cass, I'm going to cum," he said.

"No, not yet," Cassandra said. "I want to try something," she added, moving so that she now sat cross-legged on the bed, facing Lucius. "Give that to me," she demanded, holding out a hand for the vibrator. "I want to rub it over your balls when you're in my mouth."

With that, Lucius handed it over and Cassandra began rubbing the vibrator over Lucius testes as she sucked him.

"That feels great, Cass."

"Think you can hold on for a few minutes?" she asked.

"Only if you go slowly," he laughed, looking down at Cassandra as she held his erect phallus in her right hand and licked it as though she were licking an ice lollipop.

A few minutes elapsed with Cassandra taking things slowly, as Lucius had asked.

"Want to cum?" she asked.

"Yes – and I don't think I can hold back much longer," he groaned.

Chapter Nineteen

"Then cum inside me," Cassandra said, lying on her back.

"Sure," Lucius replied. "But you know you said you fantasised about two men at once?"

"Yes – what have you got planned?"

"How about me and the vibrator inside you at the same time?" he asked.

"We can give it a try," Cassandra said excitedly. "I'm going to feel pretty full what with a man with a dick as thick as yours *and* the vibrator – but let's give it a go!"

With her thighs wide open, Lucius eased the vibrator inside his lover, then slid himself in above it.

"Oh my God," Cassandra gasped. "Now fuck me," she added, frantically rubbing her clitoris with one hand as she leant her head forward and pulled her breast toward her mouth to lick her nipple, as Lucius thrust in and out of her.

"Does it feel good, you dirty bastard?" Cassandra gasped

"Yes!"

"Call me a whore," she said. "Is it buzzing against your cock and balls?"

Chapter Nineteen

"Yes, you whore" Lucius said, thrusting into Cassandra as deeply as he could.

"Oh God, I'm going to cum," gasped Cassandra.

"Me too," said Lucius, his breathing stopping for a moment before he let out a gasp, moving his mouth from Cassandra's breast to her mouth.

"I can feel it!" Cassandra said, pulling Lucius's head toward her to French kiss him.

"That was amazing," Lucius said, lying on top of Cassandra for a few minutes, before withdrawing and lying next to her.

"Thank you! I guess being a courtesan two hundred years ago taught me a thing or two," she said, giving a little giggle.

"Come here, you," Lucius said, wrapping Cassandra in his arms and kissing her.

"It's hot in here," she said.

"Yes, we're all wet and sticky," Lucius replied.

"Just the way I like it!"

The next few hours were spent blissfully naked, lying in the sun as it alighted on their bed.

Chapter Nineteen

"You've made me so happy, Lucius. I was lost until I met you," Cassandra confided.

"And you've brought me back to life," Lucius replied.

Suddenly, there was a noise outside.

"Oh God, not again," Cassandra said, sitting up in bed and pulling the sheets around her.

"Let me go and see," Lucius said, pulling on his trousers and quickly fastening them before pulling on a shirt.

"There, I heard something again," Cassandra said, getting from the bed and looking for her clothes. "Is it him?" she asked, now that Lucius was at the window.

"I'm not sure. I can't see anything that could be making a noise," he replied.

"Cassandra! Cassandra! Are you going to come back to me?" Simeon shouted. Only then was Lucius able to see him standing beneath their bedroom window.

"Yes, it's him. He's down there with a noose around his neck."

"Oh, for God's sake," Cassandra said, quickly getting dressed.

Chapter Nineteen

"If you don't come back to me, I'm going to kill myself," Simeon shouted.

"We'd better get down there and talk to him," Lucius said.

"This can't go on – I just want him to leave me alone," Cassandra said.

Within a minute, Cassandra and Lucius were downstairs. With the door unbolted, they ran around the front of the shop and turned around the corner of the house to be confronted by Simeon who, by now, had placed a ladder against a tree, climbed it, and fastened the loose end of the noose around a branch.

"So, are you going to come back to me or do I have to kill myself?" Simeon said.

"This is ridiculous – it's blackmail! If I came back to you, would I be coming back because I love you or because I don't want you doing this?"

"I can't live without you, Cass. Didn't I always treat you well?" Simeon said, raising his voice in accusation.

"No, you were horrible to me," she replied.

"You bitch!" Simeon shouted, losing his footing, and falling from the ladder.

Chapter Nineteen

"Lucius, do something!" Cassandra screamed.

Lucius raced toward the ladder and quickly climbed it.

"It's no good, I can't undo it," he said, reaching for the rope to pull Simeon back onto the ladder.

"He's turning blue," Cassandra screamed, reaching up, then jumping as if to support Simeon's feet.

Simeon thrashed about on the end of the rope as he struggled to breathe, clutching at the noose with his fingers.

Suddenly, he stopped moving and let out a guttural last breath.

"What are we doing out here?" Cassandra asked. "Whoa, who is that?" she said, pointing up at the corpse. "Quick, get him down."

"I don't know what we're doing out here. We were in bed and that's the last I remember," Lucius said, running for a knife to cut the rope by which Simeon had accidentally hung himself.

"But who is that guy?" Cassandra asked. "Is he one of the locals?"

Chapter Nineteen

"I don't know, I've never seen him before," Lucius replied. Quickly he cut the rope and Simeon fell to earth with a thud, Lucius descending the ladder before running to the corpse and turning it onto its back.

"Cass, he looks very much like the husband that murdered you."

"But you said he'd been hung," Cassandra replied, rising to her feet, and backing away from the corpse in fear.

"It's okay, Cass. I can't be it's the same man. Let's go into the village and tell the police."

"Lucius, I'm frightened," she replied.

"It's okay, Cass – everything will be fine, you'll see," he added. "Nothing will come between us, I promise."

.

Chapter Twenty

Two weeks later, Cassandra's friend Anna Harris had a visit from the police to give her an update on her missing persons' report.

"Anna Harris? I'm PC Watkins. I've come to give you an update on your missing persons' report. May I come in, please?" said the fresh-faced policeman, as Anna opened the door.

"Yes, of course. It's been two weeks and I was going to call you and find out if you had an update for me," Anna said, beckoning the policeman to enter and closing the door behind him. "Please, come in and sit down," she added, gesturing to her sofa.

"Yes, sorry it's taken a while but people aren't always missing because something has happened to them – sometimes they just want a little time to themselves. We usually give it six days before we make any enquiries."

"That seems rather a long time," Anna replied, folding her arms and leaning back in her chair.

"Well, your friend's not a child and if she just wants to up and leave then that's her decision."

Chapter Twenty

"I understand that, but I was concerned for her mental health as she was saying some very strange things when she last visited me."

"Yes, about that," the policeman said, looking at his notepad.

"What about it? Have you found her? Is she okay?" Anna asked, unfolding her arms, and leaning forward.

"No, we've not found her. In fact, the only Cassandra Wyvern we've been able to find died seventy-four years ago."

"That's ridiculous," Anna protested. "She was here just last week."

"How did she contact you to say she was going to visit?"

"She never did, she'd just turn up unannounced. We went to university together in Bristol but she only moved to Wales about a year ago when she met some man online."

"Ah yes, that would be," the policeman began, before looking at his notepad a second time.

"Simeon Danton," Anna said.

"Yes, did you know him?"

Chapter Twenty

"No, I've never met him. She'd only been with him a few weeks when the lockdown started. Why? Do you need a description?"

"No, it's just that we can find no record of anyone with that name."

"What? That's crazy!" Anna said, standing up and pacing around the room in agitation.

"I'm very sorry, Mrs Harris, but we can find no record of either your friend or her partner – at least, no one with her name in this area in the last seventy-four years – and no record at all of anyone named Simeon Danton."

"What! So they've both just disappeared and you're not going to do anything about it?" Anna queried.

"I'm sorry," the policeman said, rising to his feet. "Our enquiries indicate that the Cassandra Wyvern you knew – and her partner – never existed."

"That's crazy, they must have existed!" Anna shouted.

"No - I'm sorry. Maybe they were both using fake names."

"But I've known her for years" Anna remonstrated.

Chapter Twenty

"I'm sorry," said the policeman.

"I'll see you out," Anna's husband said, having just entered the room from the garden and seeing that the policeman was anxious to leave.

"Thank you," said the policeman.

As the two left the living room, Andrew Harris shut the living room door behind them.

"I suppose I shouldn't tell you this, but the last year has been very difficult for her."

"I understand," said the policeman. "It's not been easy for any of us."

"Yes, she lost her mother and then she began obsessing about the past and how much nicer it would be to live then than now. She then started mentioning her friend a lot."

"Ah, we can find no record of such a woman living around this area since nineteen forty-seven. Did you ever meet her friend?"

"No - Anna told me that she used to visit but it was always at times when I wasn't here. I'm not saying they're all a figment of her imagination but there's something amiss," he added.

"I hope that as the lockdown eases things improve for you," the policeman said, placing his hand on the handle of the front door now that

Chapter Twenty

Andrew Harris had removed his hand in order to talk.

"She's not well," Andrew Harris confided, as the policeman opened the front door and stepped out onto the garden path. "We've been told that the only thing that's going to help is counselling."

Chapter Twenty

Printed in Great Britain
by Amazon